# ELLE

## A TABOO TREAT

# ZO

# K WEBSTER

*Enzo*
Copyright © 2019 K Webster

Cover Design: All By Design
Photo: Adobe Stock
Editor: All About the Edits
Formatting: Champagne Book Design

Jenna's grown up in the system.
Forced to be tough, wary, and hard.

She's only been able to count on herself.
Until Enzo.
He's much older and responsible for looking after her.
What should be a job to him, evolves into much
more.

Late night phone calls.
Lingering touches.
A forbidden fire that burns brighter each day.

Everything about him exudes strength.
His will to protect her is more than she could ever
ask for.
Sadly, though, even heroes have their limitations.

But she doesn't need a hero.
She just needs him.

# dedication

Aunt P,
Sometimes people who yell the loudest have the
biggest hearts.
I miss you.

# K Webster's taboo World

Welcome to my taboo world! These stories began as an effort to satisfy the sweeter side of the taboo cravings in my reader group. The two stories in the duet, *Bad Bad Bad*, were written off the cuff and on the fly for my group. It was later deemed too hot for Amazon, but can be found on my website for purchase. Since everyone seemed to love the stories so much, I expanded the characters and the world. I've been adding new stories ever since. Each book stands alone from the others and doesn't need to be read in any particular order. I hope you enjoy the naughty characters in this town! These are quick reads sure to satisfy your craving for instalove, smokin' hot sex, and happily ever afters!

*Bad Bad Bad*
*Coach Long*
*Ex-Rated Attraction*
*Mr. Blakely*
*Malfeasance*
*Easton*
*Crybaby*
*Lawn Boys*
*Renner's Rules*
*The Glue*
*Dane*
*Enzo*

Several more titles to be released soon!
Thanks for reading!
K

*"Just let the good happen."*

# en

A TABOO TREAT

# zo

# one

*Jenna*

*Past—Fifteen years old*

"They're not going to keep you."

I look up from my book to meet the bored stare of my new foster brother, Ryder. He's thirteen going on thirty. Arrogant for a kid in the same boat as me. Motherless. Fatherless. Hopeless.

"Who says I want to be kept?"

He scowls as though just now realizing I'll never take the bait. The obnoxious kid and his little brother, Rex, seem to think I'm a threat to their happiness. Truth is, I want to stay under the radar. I'm not here to try and take the favored spot away from them. This isn't my first rodeo. Same story, different home. Over and over again. I just want to be left alone.

"They want to adopt us, but every time they start talking about it, someone shows up with another kid." He crosses his arms over his chest and frowns at me, as though this is all my fault.

I close my book and slide off the lumpy bed. I've been here six weeks and have yet to try and think of it as home. They're never home to me. Just a new place to sleep and eat. I'm simply counting down until the day I turn eighteen so I can make my own rules.

"Get out of my room," I bark out.

"Not your room," he says coolly, squaring his shoulders.

The kid may be just as tall as me, but I've gone up against kids taller, meaner, and crueler.

"Get. Out. Of. My. Room."

He shoves me. "Make me."

I fist my hands, ready to pummel this little kid, when we hear commotion downstairs. Adults talking loudly. A baby screaming. Ryder bolts, and I'm on his heels. When we reach the bottom of the stairs, he curses under his breath.

Katrina, my social worker, is talking to my foster mother, Amanda, and her husband, Blake, while holding a screaming infant in her arms. Both Amanda and Blake are stiff and nodding as Katrina somehow speaks over the crying baby to give them information. I don't make it all out, but I hear some things.

*She'll only be here a few weeks.*

*She'll get adopted fast.*

*They're heaven-sent for taking her on at the last minute.*

The screaming becomes too much and I rush back upstairs. We're not supposed to close the door, but I do it anyway. I curl up on my bed and hate the way my heart hammers in my chest. Who abandons a little baby?

Bitterness creeps up inside me.

My mom, that's who.

I was given up for adoption immediately. I've been in and out of foster homes ever since. When I was younger, I dreamed my mom had only lost me and that she'd come back for me one day. I held on to that hope for years. It's what had me acting out when people were trying to help me. I was afraid they were trying to take me before my mom could find me. Sometimes I convinced myself it was my dad who would save me—that he was always looking for his lost little girl. Around the age of thirteen, though, I realized I'd been permanently abandoned. My parents didn't want me. End of story. And every day since, I've been convincing myself I didn't want them either.

The door swings open and Blake frowns at me. "What'd we say about the door?"

I shrug. Blake and Amanda are young—in their early thirties—and somehow seem to think God called them to foster kids. They drag me to church every Sunday and Wednesday, and are quite sancti-monious, if you ask me. At church, they preen and smile humbly when people tell them how wonderful they are for fostering kids. But at home? At home, they sigh, they cry, they yell, they slam doors. I've been here six weeks and the two kids who were here before me have left. Then they got me. Now, they've got a screaming banshee.

He grumbles, but starts setting up a piece of equipment on one side of the room in front of the closet. It takes me all of a few seconds to realize it's a portable baby bed. Ughhhh, no. I do *not* want that screaming thing in my room. I can still hear it wailing downstairs.

"Katrina said she'll only be here for a few days," he explains to me, exasperation in his tone.

"Cool."

His head snaps my way and he frowns at me. Blake always wears the same look of tired disappointment. Amanda just cries.

I pick my book back up and try to concentrate, but all I can hear is the screaming baby. I wonder if they've fed it. *Her.* Babies need to eat and this one sounds starved.

"Colic," he grinds out, as if this makes sense to me. "They sent us a baby with colic."

"Cool," I utter again because I don't know why he's telling me this.

He pinches his thumb in two of the metal pieces on the baby bed and lets out a string of curse words under his breath.

*I heard those…*

The giggle that escapes me is inappropriate, and it earns me a nasty glare from Blake. As soon as he finishes with the bed, he stalks out of my room. Minutes later, the screaming gets louder as Amanda brings it—*her*—into my quiet sanctuary. The baby is flailing, red-faced, and wailing.

"Jenna, can you keep an eye on Cora until we can get everything settled with Katrina?" Amanda asks, the exhaustion already bleeding into her every word.

If she's tired fifteen minutes into this, how will she ever last a few days?

"Thanks," she clips out as she deposits the infant into the crib and pulls a diaper bag off her shoulder.

The crying doesn't let up when she leaves. I don't miss the fact that she closes the door—and breaks her own rule—behind her. From my bed, I stare across the room at the hysterical baby. Her cries are maddening, so I can hardly blame Blake and Amanda for already losing their minds. With a frustrated huff, I stand and walk over to her. I've never held a baby before so I struggle for a moment as I pull her into my arms.

It's then I smell her.

Poop.

Ughhhh.

"They left you in a messy diaper. No wonder

you're pissed," I utter to her softly. "I can help, banshee baby."

Her crying is still out of control. I'm able to tune it out as I focus on lying her down on my bed to change her. Inside her bag, I find some wipes and diapers and a few changes of clothes. It takes a long time to get all the poop off her red bottom and I'm pretty sure I got some on me, but I finally get her cleaned. Putting the clean diaper on is difficult, but I eventually figure it out. Her crying has softened some but when I start undressing her, it picks back up.

"I'm getting you out of those yucky clothes and into your jammies," I explain to her, as though she can understand. "You'll be cozy then, banshee baby."

Dressing Cora is like dressing one of the old baby dolls I used to play with, except this baby doll screams and kicks and thrashes. Eventually, I'm able to zip her up in some cute onesie jammies with yellow ducks on them.

The door opens and Amanda thrusts a warm bottle at me. "Try giving her this." Then, she leaves again, making sure to close the door behind her.

Irrational anger surges inside me. Was this how it was with me when I was a baby? Where is Cora's mother? How could she not want her baby? Tears burn in my eyes but I blink them away as I gently pick her up again. I sit down on my bed with my back against the wall and hold the bottle up.

"Is this what you want?"

Cora opens her mouth, searching, and I tilt the bottle up to offer it to her. The crying is silenced as she greedily gulps down the warm formula. Her lashes are wet with tears but now she stares at me with large, soulful blue eyes. For a second, I'm caught in her stare.

She's so beautiful.

A little angel with no wings.

"I'm sorry you're stuck with me," I tell her softly. "I'm not good at baby stuff, and unfortunately, I don't think Amanda and Blake are either." I stroke her silky blonde hair. Yep, definitely an angel. "But I'll try. While you're here the next few days, I'll make sure those dummies don't forget to feed and change you. Sound like a deal?"

I nudge her flailing fist and she grips my finger. Her blue eyes never leave mine as she drinks from her bottle. Now that she's clean and no longer screaming, I kind of like her. She's the only one who doesn't look at me as though I'm an intruder in this house. This little baby stares at me like I saved her. My heart melts.

"We could stick together," I propose, smiling at the cute baby.

She pops off the nipple, formula running down her cheek, and grins a toothless smile at me, before searching for it again.

We could stick together.

Until some nice family adopts the pretty little girl.

7

Everyone needs someone, even if it's only for a few days.

Right then, as I watch her drink, I make a silent promise to the both of us. I'm going to take care of her until they take her away. Like a little sister. I never had a sister. I never had anyone.

"You can call me Sissy," I tell her with a smile, and kiss her forehead.

She lets out a tiny sigh and I realize she's demolished her bottle. Her eyelids grow heavy and she falls asleep in my arms.

My heart stutters in my chest when I realize I don't want to let her go.

# two

My eyes droop and I try to focus on Coach Long's lecture about the Rational Zero Theorem, but it's growing more and more difficult. Last night, Cora was up all night crying. She's prone to ear infections and when she gets like she was last night, I know she has one. If it were up to me, I'd take her right in to the doctor. But it's not up to me. I have to convince my foster mother Juanita she needs to go.

Absently, I rub the bruise on my bicep. Juanita is older and uses a cane. And I don't think the cane is for actual walking. I've been hit with her stupid cane more times than I care to admit, but I'd gladly step in front of that cane every damn time to keep her from hitting Cora or the boys. Malachi and Xavier get the cane a lot, though. Cora is just small enough to hide behind one of us, thank God.

My eyes burn from lack of sleep and I yawn. I can feel myself drifting off, thinking about how hot she felt this morning.

"...factors of the leading coefficient..." Coach Long continues on.

After school, I'll need to hurry. Her pediatrician's office closes at four. I'll need time to get home from the bus, light a fire under Juanita, and get her in to be seen. She needs antibiotics.

Another yawn, so wide my eyes water.

I met Cora when she was just five months old. It's like the system paired us together after that because we bounced from home to home together. Cora and I stayed with Amanda and Blake for a few months until they informed everyone they were adopting Ryder and Rex before getting out of being foster parents for good. God was leading them to adopt, they'd said. Down another path, they'd explained. Cora and I weren't supposed to be on that path, so Katrina took us down another. Another home, another day.

I try not to think bitter thoughts toward Katrina. It's not her fault she moved to another state. Yet, she was just one more adult who abandoned us in our life. Cora and I were both assigned a new caseworker.

Lorenzo Tauber.

Closing my eyes, I can't help but think of him. Mr. Tauber is hot. No way around it. When he'd introduced himself as my new caseworker, I laughed in his face. The guy looked better suited for a freaking runway, not catering to unwanted children. He's been our caseworker for several months now, and I'd been embarrassed he was a part of the transition from our last home to Juanita's. I still remember the sad way he looked at me. As though, for once in my life, someone might care enough to do something permanently helpful in my life.

But then he left. Dropped Cora and I off with only a few words of encouragement. As though his words would fix everything.

*"Hang in there."*

I let out a derisive snort that earns me a warning glare from Coach Long. Several students snigger at my outburst.

Tauber was wrong though. His words didn't do a damn thing. He'd left us with Juanita and her stupid cane.

My head throbs slightly and I rub at my temples, closing my eyes. One day—only a couple of months from now—I'm going to turn eighteen and I'll get us out of this place. I'll adopt Cora and we'll move someplace happy. She can have all the cookies she wants and will never be told no. We'll spend our days swinging, chasing crickets, and singing songs.

"Detention, Miss Pruitt. After school."

I blink open my eyes and gape up at the man

glowering down at me. "W-What?"

"You seem to think laughing in my class and then sleeping through it are acceptable. Not in my class," he snarls, before storming back to the front of the classroom.

Tears threaten and I sit up abruptly. I can't stay after school. I have to get back to Juanita and convince her to take Cora to the doctor. This is terrible timing.

If we miss seeing the doctor today, Cora's temperature will keep spiking. She'll scream endlessly in pain. This can all be avoided if these adults would wake the hell up. A tear streaks down my cheek and I hastily swipe it away. One girl named Winter frowns at me. She's usually the troublemaker in Coach's class. I may have a mouth on me sometimes, but I don't ever jeopardize my time with Cora.

"Are you okay?" she whispers to me.

I nod and bite on my lip to keep from crying as the bell rings and everyone stands up. Winter hands me a piece of paper with her phone number on it. I don't have the heart to tell her I don't have a cell phone or access to one. Instead, I fold it and tuck it into my ratty black hoodie.

Coach Long ignores me as he stalks over to his desk. As soon as the room empties out, I stand and rush over to him.

"C-Coach," I start, my voice hoarse with emotion. "Please don't give me detention. I—"

"The crying act doesn't work with me," he says in a cold tone, not making eye contact as he flips through some papers.

"Please," I cry out, "you can't do this."

His glare snaps to me. "This is my classroom, Miss Pruitt. You sleep and goof off, you get detention. I told you this from day one. It's not a secret."

Defeated, I take a step back, hating the way my chin wobbles wildly. My hands tremble as panic surges up inside me. She needs to go to the doctor after school. Maybe I can call Juanita and convince her over the phone. I'm frantic as I clumsily stuff my things into my bag. The shaking in my hands won't stop, nor will the choked sounds leaving me. When I stand up and shoulder my backpack, Coach is watching me with furled brows.

"What's going on?" he demands.

"I have to take her to the doctor," I admit with a sob. "My foster mom is impossible to deal with and Cora has an ear infection. She needs antibiotics."

His gaze softens. "Your sister?"

*My everything.*

"Yeah."

He purses his lips and looks away. I can tell his wheels are turning. "You were up all night with her."

I blink at him in surprise. "Yeah, how'd you know?"

Amusement glimmers in his eyes. "Lucky guess."

Then, he sighs in frustration. "No one gets out of detention."

My head bows. "I know."

"But I'm not a total monster, like everyone thinks. Take care of your sister, get some sleep, and pay attention in class," he grumbles. "You're a senior. You need good grades if you're going to get out there and make something of yourself."

I press my lips together and pray my cheeks aren't turning red. Sometimes I hate that the teachers all know my situation. That I'm a foster kid. Alone and unloved and at an unfair advantage.

"Thanks," I mutter. "I'll do my best."

"Get out of here," he says as kids start piling into class for the next hour.

I can hear her screams the moment I step off the bus. An ache that's been deep in my bones seems to flare into agonizing pain.

*I'm coming, banshee baby.*

Running past other kids that have come off the bus, I rush to Juanita's house. It's in desperate need of repair, but she never does it. She never does anything except chain smoke and watch stupid talk shows all day. When we get home, we're her evening entertainment and her exercise as she whaps us with her cane.

Poor Cora has to put up with her all day while we're at school.

The moment I burst inside the door, I toss my backpack to the floor and follow the screams. In the living room, the television is blaring.

"She has an ear infection," I bark out over the noise. "Call her pediatrician."

Juanita ignores me to light another cigarette.

"Juanita!" I bellow. "Call Dr. Powell."

"Girl, you need to watch your tone with me," she bites back, her eyes never leaving the screen.

I storm into the living room and turn off the television. "Call him now, or I call Mr. Tauber."

Juanita grabs for her cane and I take a step back, even though I'm well out of reach. "She's just a fussy brat. You spoil her, girl."

I cross my arms and glower at her. Cora's screams are my undoing but I won't budge until Juanita makes the call. Finally, she gives in and calls in our little emergency. As soon as I hear her confirm we'll be there in half an hour, I rush upstairs to my baby.

Bursting through our bedroom door, I find her standing in the middle of the room. Her blonde hair is sweaty and messy. Snot is running down her lips and chin. She's red-faced and sick. My poor, poor baby.

"Cora," I choke out, rushing over to her. I pull her into my arms and kiss her sweaty head. Her entire body trembles as she clings to me. "Shhhh," I coo as I pat her back. "We're going to see the doctor and get you all better."

There's no calming her when she gets this way. My guess is she has a double ear infection. Her skin is so hot and she's clearly in a lot of pain. Cora is susceptible to chronic ear infections. I wish they'd go on and do the tubes in her ears like Dr. Powell mentioned to our last foster family.

While holding Cora, I pack her little pink backpack with some of her favorite things. The zipper doesn't work and it's times like these I wish I had money to provide for her. I'd buy her a newer and bigger backpack to hold more of her comfort items.

Once we're packed, I carry her downstairs and out the front door. Juanita begrudgingly follows, her cane whapping the floor as she walks. With each crack to the floor, Cora jumps.

"It's okay," I whisper into her hair. "She won't hit us outside that house."

I buckle Cora into her seat and sit beside her in the back. Juanita drives like the old granny she is, rolling through stop signs, nearly sideswiping other cars, and driving at least ten below the posted limit. When we finally pull into the doctor's office, I unbuckle her and rush inside.

"Hi, Jenna," the receptionist named Lori says. I like Lori. She's a friendly woman with purple hair and a nose ring. I love that she posts pictures of her children all along the wall beside her desk. All six of them look happy. I wish she had room for two more.

"Hey, Lori. Cora needs antibiotics."

"Sure thing, hon. Dr. Powell will get her fixed up." When Juanita waddles through the door, Lori's smile fades and her glare is icy.

I leave Juanita to handle checking her in and sit down with Cora in my lap. She's no longer screaming, and just whimpering. When she's upset, she twists my hair in her fingers and rubs it on her face. And when she's been crying, I end up with snot all in my hair. But as long as she's calmed down, I don't care. I'll wash it later.

Eventually, we're called back and thankfully, Juanita opts to stay in the waiting room. I let out a sigh of relief as we wait for Dr. Powell.

Nurse Lou walks in and smiles gently at us. Lou is old like Juanita but wonderful. Her pockets are always filled with stickers and candy.

Cora sits up and grins at Lou. "Sucker?"

Lou plucks out a pink sucker from her pocket and unwraps it. Cora happily pops the sucker in her mouth. She's still hot and in pain, but she's better. Cora may only be two, but she knows this is a safe place where they always fix her up. Lou buzzes about checking her temperature—one hundred and one point seven—and her blood pressure. She taps away on the computer and then leaves us to wait for Dr. Powell.

The white-haired man eventually shows up and frowns. He asks us the normal questions at first, about her health, and then about our home situation. I give him the generic answers, hoping for him to hurry and prescribe her the medication so she will feel better.

"Does your foster mother ever hit you?" Dr. Powell asks, his attention darting back and forth between us.

I freeze and Cora nods.

"Cane hurts Sissy," Cora whispers.

Dr. Powell glances at me sadly. "I'll call for Lou. I'm obligated to examine you both and call your caseworker."

I steel myself so I don't cry and give him a clipped nod. "Whatever."

After an embarrassing twenty minutes of Lou and Dr. Powell documenting our bruises, mostly mine, we redress and wait for Mr. Tauber.

I just want Cora to get antibiotics in her.

The rest can wait.

# three

*Enzo*

I was about to head out for the day when I got the call from Dr. Powell. Two of my kids, Jenna Pruitt and Cora Wells, were brought in to see him. Their foster mother has been abusing them and, after some careful questioning, also two of the other boys at the home. So, instead of meeting my mom and dad at Red Lobster for an early dinner, I'm on my way to meet with Sheriff McMahon and Dr. Powell.

When I pull in at the doctor's office, I watch with a little too much glee as an officer assists a handcuffed Juanita Aikens into the back of a squad car. For every good foster family, there are too many bad ones. I try like hell before I place these kids to find them some-place safe, but some slip under the radar until it's too late. Nothing makes you feel like a failure more than having to rescue kids from a home you put them in.

I walk inside and am guided into the breakroom where the girls are waiting. Cora is asleep in Jenna's arms. Jenna, with dark circles under her eyes, stares up at the ceiling, as though she herself might be seconds from passing out. My heart aches at seeing these two. When I'd been given their cases, I'd felt sorry for them. They're not actual siblings, but Katrina left notes before she moved to treat them as they were because it went smoother that way.

Dr. Powell shakes my hand and then we discuss the physical abuse observations. Jenna and Cora both admitted that Juanita hit them and the Bryant boys a lot. I have four kids to move tonight. Scrubbing my face in frustration, I rack my brain for answers I don't have at the moment. My stomach grumbles and I ignore it.

I make some calls and am happy to see the nurses have ordered some pizza. Jenna eats some but Cora continues to sleep. Probably best for the sick child. I steal a piece of pizza as I make some calls. There's a family who can take all four. Don and Barb Friedman. They don't have any negative marks to speak of, and only one kid in their charge. So, I make the arrangements.

"Time to go," I tell Jenna. "We have to pick up the boys and your things. The Friedmans can take you all in until we can sort out something better."

Jenna's green eyes flash with anger. "There's never anything better. In fact, it just gets worse."

Guilt burns a hole in my gut. "Hang in there."

"I hate when you say that," she seethes, pushing past me.

I'm frowning after her when Dr. Powell taps me on the shoulder, handing me a bag of medication.

"Make sure the new house is non-smoking. Smoking isn't good for Cora's allergies," he says.

"I'll do my best." Not a lie. I always do my best. It's just never good enough. I can tell the foster parents not to smoke in the house until I'm blue in the face, and they'll light up the moment my car leaves the driveway.

I follow the girls out to the car, giving Sheriff McMahon a wave on the way out. Once we're settled, the girls in the back and myself up front, I drive them toward Juanita's.

"We need to stop by the pharmacy to get her medication," Jenna instructs, her eyes burning into the rearview mirror, challenging me to say no.

"Dr. Powell must have sent someone to pick it up. I've got them."

All anger bleeds from Jenna and she sags in relief. She leans over and kisses Cora on the head. I watch them every time I stop at a light. Poor fucking kids.

We eventually arrive at Juanita's and I escort them inside. Another caseworker named Seth sits on the sofa, asking the Bryant boys some questions. I give him a wave and follow Jenna into the kitchen. I rip open the bag of medicine and open the antibiotics bottle.

Cora stirs awake in Jenna's arms and starts whining. "Yuckyuckyuck."

"Gotta take it, Cora," I urge gently.

Cora screeches, shaking her head. "Noooo!"

"Heyyy," Jenna says in a calm tone that settles Cora. "Drink it up, and your ears will stop hurting. Do it for Sissy."

The toddler doesn't seem pleased and after I pour the pink foul-smelling medicine into the cup, Jenna takes it and offers it Cora. Cora cries a little but with some gentle coaxing, Jenna gets her to swallow it down. The moment she does, Jenna relaxes.

We spend the next half hour packing up the kids. Between Seth and I, it doesn't take long to gather their meager belongings. More stabs of guilt in my heart. More painful memories I like to keep pushed away.

I, just like these poor kids, was a kid left to rot in the system.

But unlike me, they didn't have angels swoop in and save them.

Mom and Dad adopted me when I was just nine. I'd gone from damn near starving, severely beat on by other kids in the home, and so goddamn lonely, to happy. Mom and Dad, and their son, Elijah, were my happily ever after. They were my heroes. Still are.

The guilt that I found a forever home and these kids never do, never ceases to end.

While Seth settles the boys at the Friedmans' house, I help Jenna set up the portable toddler bed. Cora is snoring now but no longer has a terrible temperature. Jenna seems ready to fall asleep where she stands. I move the sleeping child from the twin bed to the toddler bed, thankfully without waking her.

"Call me if things get bad here," I tell Jenna, handing her one of my cards.

She tucks it away in her hoodie. "Right, I'll get right on that because the ones who abuse us then let us use their phones to tattle on them."

Her bottom lip quivers and tears cling to her lashes but don't fall. This brave girl can barely keep it together. In a move that shocks us both, I pull her to me and hug her. She's stiff but then releases a choked sob. Her fingers clutch my shirt on the sides as she cries against my chest. We're not supposed to get close to these kids. At least, that's how we're trained. But I remember being a young kid and desperately needing a hug from someone—anyone. Right now, Jenna needs a hug. She's falling apart before my very eyes, and it fucking guts me.

*Hang in there.*

My go-to phrase.

It's on the tip of my tongue.

What a line of bullshit. If someone would have told me that when I was a boy, I'd have kicked them in the nuts. There's no hanging in there. A better phrase would be, "Don't drown." Life is going to try to push you under the water—stand on you, smashing you to the ground way down below. It's dark and cold, and you'll feel as though you're suffocating. You'll be alone. So fucking alone. Don't drown.

I stroke my fingers through Jenna's hair. They become tangled at the bottom where it's crusted with something. Snot probably. Cora likes to rub her face all in Jenna's hair when she's needing comfort.

"Find a way to call me. At school, if you have to. I want to know if there's a problem at the first sign of trouble. Finding out that Juanita has been beating on you guys for months now is unacceptable," I chide. "I can't help you if you don't tell me."

She stiffens and pulls away. "Got it."

"Get some sleep," I order, pointing to the bed.

She kicks off her shoes and falls onto the mattress without another word. Within seconds, she's sleeping heavily like her foster sister. For a long while, I stand, staring at them as they sleep. Why is life so cruel to sad, innocent kids?

They need a hero.

"They don't let us eat," Jenna whispers. "They keep the food locked away."

They've been at the Friedmans' for days, and I'm already getting calls about how terrible they are. Fuck.

"They starve you?" I ask, blinking away sleep as I roll over to check the time. Three in the morning. What the hell?

"They try," she hisses. "I sneak into their room and take Don's key."

"Have they hurt you?"

She's silent for a beat. "Aside from trying to starve everyone, not physically."

"I'm sorry, Jenna, but this isn't dire enough for me to do anything about." Cold, hard truth. At three in the morning, apparently, I'm a dick.

"I hate you. I hate you all."

She hangs up and the guilt swallows me whole.

Don Friedman is the only one home when I do an unofficial surprise home check the next day. They're out of school for winter break now, but there are no sounds of a normal home. No cartoons playing. No kids running through the house. No one in the kitchen making a snack, or any sign the kids are even there. Just silence.

"Where are the kids?" I ask in a bland tone despite the fury that is welling inside me.

"Playing in their rooms."

"I'm going to talk to them." I walk past him to the stairwell. He follows me. I don't like this asshole. Tall and bulky, like maybe he used to play football back in his prime, but now he's just fattened up, yet never lost the ego.

First, I check on the boys. Malachi is lying on the bed, reading. Xavier is playing with plastic dinosaurs on the floor. Another boy named Joseph is watching Xavier play. Definitely not a dire situation. I close the door and then step across the hall to the girls' room. When I twist the handle, it's locked.

"What'd I tell you about locking this door?" Don demands from behind me.

Silence.

"Jenna, it's me," I say through the door.

Footsteps can be heard and then the lock disengages. She cracks open the door and I see one fierce green eye through the opening. Relief glimmers in that one eye as she steps away, granting us entry.

I turn to tell Don he's not needed when I catch him staring at Jenna in a way that makes my hackles rise. Hungrily. Like he wants to have a little taste. When he notices my scowl, he smirks and leaves the room, closing the door behind him. I flit my gaze over Jenna's appearance. She's not wearing much—a pair of cotton shorts that reveal her pale legs and a long-sleeved sweater that leaves little to the imagination as it hangs off one shoulder, revealing her bare skin.

"You can't dress like that around him," I tell her irritably.

"Like what?" Her green eyes are wide and innocent.

Fuck.

I scrub my palm down my face. "Grown men like him don't need to see you barely clothed. A lot of creeps in the world."

"Creeps," Cora parrots from the floor where she scribbles in a coloring book.

A ghost of a smile dances across Jenna's lips. I'd love to see her truly smile with happiness.

"Just wear more clothes around him," I grumble, chasing away her smile, as I toss her hoodie at her.

She pulls it on and scowls at me. "Not like I have tons of choices on what to wear." The bitterness in her tone stabs at me.

I sigh and sit on the end of her bed. Cora scoots away from me, eyeing me warily. She looks tons better, which makes me grateful.

"How are things going? Are they giving you food?"

"Exactly enough and not a morsel more." She sits

beside me, cross-legged on the bed. "Certainly not dire."

I turn to regard her. Up close, I can see a few freckles on her nose and cheeks. Mostly, I can see the fire in her eyes. She's definitely too pretty—a nearly eighteen-year-old girl—to be prancing around with no bra on around leering old men.

Like me?

I almost laugh at that thought. I'm not some sicko who checks out kids.

"I was tired when I said that, but I certainly didn't mean for it to sound that way," I assure her. "I just meant that it's not that easy for me to yank you out of here and move you. There has to be some semblance of proof of neglect or abuse. Lots of hoops to jump through. I'm not even here officially."

Jenna grits her teeth, stealing a glance at Cora. "So, they can starve us, just not touch us. Got it."

Thoughts of Don "touching" her boil my blood. "He even thinks about touching you and he'll regret it," I snarl. "Either of you."

Jenna's cheeks turn pink and she stares at me with her lips parted. Yep, too pretty. Too fucking pretty to be in this house with Don and his lingering stares.

"I'm sorry," she utters before launching herself at me.

The hug I'd so freely and stupidly given her the other day was clearly permission for her to do it back.

I'm stunned as she embraces me in a way that feels familiar and warm. I'm even further stunned that I squeeze her back.

"Nothing to be sorry for." My words are firm and yield no room for argument.

"I, uh, I…" Her voice cracks.

"Yeah?"

The silence stretches on. Like she wants to tell me more, but refrains. It unnerves me. I don't like the vibe here, but I can't go on hunches. I need more.

"Never mind," she mumbles, her voice tired and defeated.

"Call me if you need to," I remind her before pulling away and standing. I squat and ruffle Cora's hair. "Bye, kiddo."

Cora squawks and runs over to Jenna, who pulls her into her lap and gives me a small wave.

I leave with a heavy heart. Everything in me screams to turn around and help them. Help them from what, though? My instincts aren't enough. I need more. Once I'm in my car, I pull out my laptop and do some research on Don and Barb. Nothing concrete, but I don't get a good feeling. I call my attorney friend, Nick.

"Hello?"

I growl out my words. "Something's not right." More like everything. Everything about their situation is sketchy. I don't fucking like it one bit.

"The boys?"

"Not just the boys. Cora and Jenna too. I did some digging, and this couple is friends with Juanita Aikens." Bad people tend to stick together.

He's silent for a moment, and then I can hear the strain in his voice when he says, "What do we do?"

"I was hoping you'd know," I tell him.

I can't pull them. Not on the basis of a teenager's claim they don't feed them and the creepy way he looked at Jenna. It's not enough. But I still don't like it, the way he looked at her. Call it a hunch.

"Let me talk to August and see what we can do," he replies with a heavy sigh.

I hope whatever it is, it's enough.

I'm tired of letting these kids down.

# four

*Jenna*

As soon as Mr. Tauber leaves, I lock the door again. I'm not leaving it to chance. I've caught Don in here in the middle of the night, staring at me, and once, he entered the bathroom while I was showering to "put the towels away."

I should have told Mr. Tauber.

*Lorenzo.*

But what could he have done? He's already said unless it's something big, there's nothing he can do. Defeated, I sink down on the bed, wishing I could sleep until my birthday. Then, Cora and I can get the hell out of here.

"Book," Cora whines, shoving a picture book in my face.

I smile at her and we settle on my bed. She snuggles against me, playing with my hair.

"This book is called *My Mommy*," I say, keeping the tightness out of my voice. The last thing she needs to learn about are mommies. Mommies are weak and leave their children when times get tough. Both of our mommies sucked.

"My mommy is nice. My mommy likes rice," I read in a cheerful voice. "My mommy sings a song about the sun. My mommy is a lot of fun."

Cora looks up at me and beams her adorable toothy grin.

"My mommy feeds me lunch. My mommy likes to munch…on cookies."

Cora giggles. "Cookies!"

"My mommy washes my face. My mommy cleans all over the place."

She snuggles up against me. "My mommy is Jenna."

I freeze at her words. "I'm Sissy."

"Mommy," she argues, her cute nose scrunching.

"Uhhh, do you want to find a different book?" I ask.

She shakes her head. "Mommy book, Mommy!"

"Cora," I say firmly. "I'm Sissy."

"Mommy! Mommy!" she wails, and begins throwing a tantrum. The book gets kicked to the floor as she kicks and squirms. "Mommy! Mommy!"

"Shhh, banshee baby, shhh. You're going to make mean old Don come in here," I chide, hugging her to me.

"Mommy," she sobs. "My mommy."

I let out a heavy sigh, blinking back the tears. "In our room, you can call me Mommy. Is that better?"

She nods, another sweet grin plastered on her teary face.

"Other people might not like it if you call me Mommy, so it's our secret, okay?"

Her little head nods again, and I kiss her silky hair. One day, I'm going to legally make this kid mine. Then, no one will ever be able to separate us. She can call me Mommy all she wants when that time comes.

"Want to go play with Malachi and Xavier and Joseph?"

She gives one long look at her book on the floor before conceding to give it up to go play with the boys.

Come on, eighteen…stop taking so freaking long to get here.

I leave Cora in the room with the boys so I can catch up on homework. Coach Long's Precalculus class is killing me, but I need to pass his class with an A if I have any hope getting into a college I want. I'm deep in thought when Don steps in my room.

"What did you say to him?" he demands.

I arch a brow at him. "That you're a creep," I taunt, loving the way his eyes flare with fury. "That you watch me in the shower." I laugh cruelly at him.

"Sick pervert."

It's a lie, but I want him to know I'm not some weak girl who will take his gross advances. Too many girls and boys in the system have been taken advantage of by adults and older kids. I'll be damned if this guy thinks he can do the same to me.

"Liar," he snarls. "You're such a liar. If that were true, he wouldn't have left here without so much as a word." His eyes narrow. "But he looked unsettled, which means you said something to him. I don't like it. I won't have some skanky girl trying to fuck up my world because she wants to screw her caseworker."

"Fuck you," I hiss out at him, careful to keep my voice low so that the kids don't hear.

Lightning quick, he pounces on me. The back of his hand strikes me across the side of my face, sending me tumbling onto the bed. I jerk my gaze his way and hold my palm to the now-throbbing pain on my cheek.

"You hit me," I accuse, my eyes turning watery and my lip wobbling.

His stare falls to my bare legs and he licks his lips. "You fell."

"Leave me alone." My words are firm and fierce but the delivery falls flat due to the quiver in my voice.

"You don't make up stories that aren't true to tattle to Mr. Hero Man. Got it?"

When I don't say anything, he nods his head

toward the door. "Cora," he calls out, his eyes still on mine. Threatening.

"I got it," I bark out. "I won't say anything because nothing happened."

He smiles at me, a mouth full of yellow teeth. I can't help but shudder. "Good girl."

Cora toddles in the room and runs past him, straight into my arms. My heart hammers in my chest. I felt his unspoken threat. If I mess with him, he'll mess with me through her. I'd die before I let that happen.

I wake from a nap with Cora to the sounds of Don and Barb yelling from downstairs. They're calling for us. Maybe we get to leave. With a little too much excitement, I throw on some jeans and shoes before scooping up a sleepy-eyed Cora and heading downstairs. The boys are all waiting there, huddled together as though they have safety in numbers. I'm thankful Malachi is here to look after the other two boys. He's much younger than me but has a good head on him. It's amazing how fast you have to grow up when you're responsible for younger kids.

"'Nana," Cora whines, her hand twisting wildly in my hair.

"I'll see if I can get you a banana later," I promise.

I'll try, even if I have to walk my butt down to the store and steal one.

"Children," Barb barks, making Cora jump.

I hug her tight to me and pat her back. She's been on antibiotics for a few days, but still isn't one hundred percent herself.

"Your caseworker is on his way for a house check. I want you all on your best behavior," Don explains, his eyes boring a hole straight into me. "We don't need you all telling them any fibs."

Everyone nods, myself included.

He opens his mouth to speak again when someone knocks. Barb opens the door to Lorenzo and Seth. Both wear matching grim expressions.

"You may go to your rooms now," Barb says coolly.

"Cora would like a banana," I bite back, pinning her with a challenging stare.

"'Nana," Cora agrees softly.

"I'm hungry too," Joseph whines.

Lorenzo nods and points toward the kitchen. "We can start in the kitchen."

Barb shoots me a scathing glare but I ignore her to walk beside Lorenzo.

"You okay?" he whispers along the way.

My throat is tight with emotion. All I can do is shrug and look away from his probing hazel eyes. I sit with Cora in my lap at the kitchen table and watch with smug satisfaction as Barb and Don explain why there are locks on the refrigerator and pantry door. While Cora happily scarfs down a banana, I notice Lorenzo's brows deepen with every passing minute and he does a lot of scribbling on his clipboard.

This may not be dire as he calls it, but it's not right. I hope whoever the powers that be are agree with me and get us the hell out of here.

They're here for hours. I end up putting Cora to bed and sit near my window to try and focus on my book. Eventually, Lorenzo comes up to interview me. I can hear Seth talking to the boys across the hall.

"Can you close the door?" I plead. The last thing I want is Don overhearing.

He nods and then sits on my bed. His chocolate curls are a mess on top of his head, like he's been spending his time running his fingers through them over and over again. It makes me want to smooth them out for him. My fingers twitch to do just that. Instead, I fist my hands and wait for him to speak.

"What happened between this morning and now?" he asks, his voice soft and concerned.

I blink back tears. "Nothing dire."

He rolls his eyes and for a moment, it makes him seem so young. "Don't be like that, Jenna. I'm trying to help." He lets out a sigh and puts his clipboard down on the night stand. "Talk to me."

"Mr. Tauber," I start, absently rubbing my sore cheek.

"Enzo."

Our eyes meet and warmth swims in his gaze.

"Enzo," I amend, loving the way his shortened name rolls off my tongue. "I hate it here."

"You hate all the places."

A tear races down my cheek. "I just don't want anything to happen to Cora." The reminder of how Don looked at her earlier sends a chill of dread racing down my spine. I shudder and choke out a sob.

"Hey," Enzo rumbles. "Hey. Come here."

I fall into his embrace, desperate to not feel so alone in this world. I'm not one for letting people in. Cora is the only person I've truly loved, but it's nice that Enzo is trying to help. And not in the same way Katrina helped. With Enzo, he cares more than he's supposed to. I like that about him. I need someone to care about me. More than some obligation, but because they want to.

"Talk to me," he urges, his voice soft. He doesn't let me go but instead holds me tight, like I might break apart at any moment.

The words tumble from my lips. All the things I'd wanted to say to him earlier about Don. How he's a creep lying in wait. Then, how he hit me.

As soon as I tell him, he pulls away to look at my face. His hazel eyes search my flesh, anger glinting in them. When he gently grips my jaw to turn my head to the side, my skin heats and butterflies dance in my stomach. I know he's inspecting me for injury, but it feels so intimate. I welcome his sweet touch.

"Here?" His voice is hoarse and strained as he runs his thumb along the bruised flesh.

"Yeah."

"There's no bruise but it's red." He closes his eyes for a moment and his jaw clenches. "I'm sorry, Jenna."

More hot tears leak down my cheeks. I'm once again pulled into his embrace. He smells good and feels strong. Someone like him could keep all these creeps away. The thought is alarming but not un-wanted. I don't want to put hope in another person to save me, but for once, I don't get a choice. It's just there. Hope bubbling all over the place.

After some time, he lets out a heavy sigh. "I have to leave."

Dejected, I pull away and hastily swipe away my tears. I don't break often, but lately, it's all I've been doing. Freedom is so close I can taste it, which makes all the rest of this so much more frustrating. "I know."

"I'm working on it. I promise. Just…" He frowns and looks away. "Just don't drown until I can throw you a lifebuoy."

"No more 'hang in there'?" I ask, a smile tugging

at my lips.

He smirks. "I'm not sure I can trust you not to *hang* Donnie Boy in there if I toss you a rope instead."

"Thank you, Enzo."

He reaches forward and gently touches my sore cheek. "I want nothing more than to make sure you're safe and provided for." Our eyes meet, and then he drops his hand away before leaving without another word.

I stare at the closed door long after he's gone, praying that he's true to his word.

# five

*Enzo*

*Christmas Eve*

Today, I made a decision. An unethical one. I bought her a phone. But I need a way to make sure she's okay. Leaving those kids last night, especially the always-strong-but-severely-broken Jenna, was the hardest damn thing I've ever had to do. I'm too attached.

As I drive to the Friedmans' to meet my friend Nick, and another attorney, Dane, I call Mom. She answers on the first ring.

"Hey, baby boy," she greets, and then yells at my dad, telling him he's cutting the ham all wrong.

I smile because my parents bicker all the time. All the time. But it's almost like it's a game to them—something they play—because the love is always shining in their eyes. I remember being nine years old, in the back of their station wagon, flinching when they were arguing over where they'd take me for my first dinner. Mom wanted steak. Dad argued kids like Showbiz Pizza better because of the games. My new brother Elijah sided with Dad. I'd sat tense as hell, waiting for him to strike my new mom. Instead, she laughed as she conceded and then told everyone they owed her a fancy steak dinner. It took some getting used to but the playful banter was all it was. Playful. Silly arguments over nothing. I learned to not take life so seriously and began to relax.

"Hey, Mom."

"When are you getting here?"

I let out a heavy sigh. "Unofficial home check. I'll come over later when I finish up. Tell Eli not to eat all the damn ham before I get there."

She cackles. "You know I can't promise such a thing. That boy eats like his father."

We chat about plans for tomorrow and the weather and other unimportant shit, but it calms me. Mom has always calmed me when I'm upset. I may not be her blood, but she has that mom intuition down pat.

"You going to tell me what's up, Enzo?"

I let out a heavy sigh. "Do you ever feel helpless? Like you wish you could do more but you just can't?"

The sounds from my brother and dad disappear as Mom goes somewhere quiet. All amusement is gone. "Sometimes, son, yes."

"I just wish…" I groan and run my fingers

through my hair that is still wet from snowflakes from when I got into my car. "I just wish I could fix their situation. The kids just want happiness."

"One kid in particular?" she asks, once again always knowing exactly what's going on inside my head.

"She breaks my heart," I admit.

"I know what you mean," she murmurs. "All you can do is your best. What you're capable of. You're not a superhero. No one is. You help the kids—the girl—as best as you can. Will it be enough? Probably not. But the fact that you try is enough."

We're quiet for a moment and then I ask the question I've always wondered. "Why did you choose me? There were two of us who desperately needed help. You chose only me, Mom."

What about Logan?

Logan has been sitting in the state penitentiary for twenty years, and I can't help but think if she'd have chosen us both, maybe he'd have taken a different path. One that didn't involve violence.

"Oh, sweetie," she says sadly. "Your father and I talked a lot about you two boys. We could have handled another child, but something wasn't right. I could just feel it. Giving him a home and family were not going to simply fix him. Your father and I weren't equipped to deal with a child like Logan. We both knew it. As sad as it was to tear you two apart, it was the only thing we could do."

My jaw clenches as I think about Logan. He was my foster brother when we were kids. Like Jenna and Cora, we bounced together as though we were blood-related. Logan was always disturbed. His eyes were always cold. Always. The only times they showed warmth were for me. He got in a lot of fights with both kids and adults. When we were both nine, right before I was adopted out, he was already smoking pot and stealing liquor, where I barely even knew what that stuff was.

"Yeah," is all I can reply with. "I just got to the Friedmans'. I will see you later."

"Love you, Enzo. Always have."

"Love you too, Mom."

I pull in the driveway and wait in my car for Dane and Nick to show up. The phone in my pocket feels like both a blessing and a curse. I'm breaking the rules to give one of my kids a phone. A phone that is linked to me because it's on my cell phone plan. It's just asking for trouble. But when I walked into the store and got it set up, I wasn't thinking about my job. I was thinking about Jenna. I promised her a lifebuoy. This is her way to keep from drowning.

A pair of headlights shine behind me. I climb out of the car, shuddering against the cold and snow, and walk over to shake hands with Nick and Dane.

"You must be Nick. Pleased to finally meet you," I say to my friend dressed in a Santa suit and whom I've only conversed with over the phone.

"Nick," Dane says. "Meet Lorenzo Tauber. Enzo, this is St. Nick."

We all chuckle, but then grow serious when our gazes all end up on the house with the sad, lonely kids inside.

"And they're expecting us?" Nick asks, fidgeting as though he's nervous.

"They're expecting a visit from Santa and some gifts. The foster mom wasn't keen on a visit from the caseworker two days this week, but I convinced her this was something we do often and not part of the home study," I tell him. It's technically been more than two days but Nick and Dane don't need to know the accounts of my "unofficial" visits. "We need to tread lightly." I grip Nick's shoulder and frown. "It's easy to get angry when we see injustices done to these kids. But for us to protect them and help them, we have to remain cool. I'm trusting you by taking you here with me."

He nods at me and then they both head for the trunk to get the gifts. I grip the phone in my pocket, nerves eating me alive. Like it might go off and everyone will know I'm bringing Jenna a phone. My hand shakes slightly as I ring the doorbell.

I won't give it to her.

Decision made.

My job will be safe and I won't be doing something

that seems sketchy, like trying to communicate with a teenager. I'm sure the cops would think I was just as creepy as Don. Thank fuck he won't be here tonight, according to Barb when I called earlier to set this up.

Barb answers the door and eyes the guys behind me suspiciously as they walk up.

"Mrs. Friedman, thank you for allowing us to come," I say icily to her. This witch locks up her food and lets her husband watch little girls while they shower. I hate that I have to be nice to her, but I know the rules. Until the judge goes over the reports and makes a decision, they're stuck here, and I'll be damned if I make it harder on these kids by being an asshole to their caretaker.

"Not like I had a choice," she grumbles.

We follow her inside. The house is chilly tonight, which makes my blood boil. It makes me think of Mom, who is probably hollering at Elijah or Dad to stoke the fire because it's not warm enough. If Mom were here, she'd teach these assholes how to parent the right way.

Nick is frowning as he takes in the environment. The stale smell of smoke. The chilly air. The lack of Christmas decorations. He and Dane exchange a weighted look. It's surprising to them, but all too familiar to me.

"Kids! Get down here now!" Barb yells up the stairs.

I clench my jaw and walk over to the far corner of the living room. This isn't about me being here on an official check. It's so those kids can have a tiny moment of a happy Christmas. I wish we could do more, but this is all we can do for now.

Nick sits in the recliner, all decked out as Santa Claus, and I can't help but shoot the poor guy a reassuring smile and a wink. I like that he cares. It's always good to have an attorney as a friend when you're dealing with kids and needing judges to make shit happen.

I sense her before I see her and jerk my head over to the stairs. Jenna, wearing a fierce and untrusting mask, holds Cora tightly to her as she descends the stairs.

"Jenna," I greet, my voice rough with emotion. The desire to snatch both girls up and take them home with me is overwhelming. "Hi there, Cora." Cora hides from me like always, burying her face in Jenna's hair, and I can't help but feel dejected.

"Boys!" Barb bellows. "Get down here now! We have company!"

Jenna and Cora both flinch and I start toward them. To do what? Rescue them? I can't do shit. Not legally anyway. All I can do is make sure they see Santa and receive their presents. And then, hopefully the judge will move them out of this house where they think it's fucking fine to lock the food away and leer at Jenna.

All three boys eventually emerge from upstairs. Jenna and Cora stand close enough I can almost draw them in for a hug. Nick, thankfully, takes control of the situation and plays his role well as Santa. While everyone is distracted, watching Joseph talk to Santa and receive his gifts, I take the moment to talk to Jenna.

"How are you holding up?" I ask quietly.

She shrugs and kisses Cora's head. "We're fine."

"Staying afloat?"

A small smile tugs at her lips. "Barely, but yes."

"Jenna, take Cora over there," Barb snaps, jerking us from our private conversation.

Jenna glowers at her but walks over to Nick. She is young, but the system has aged her. Forced her to grow up a long time ago. As she holds Cora protectively to her, she reminds me of a mother bear. Claws and teeth bared, ready to tear out the throats of anyone who might try to hurt her cub. My chest aches for them. It reminds me too much of Logan. He was my family like Cora is hers. Sometimes life takes our made-up families away too.

Life fucking sucks.

Cora starts squealing when she realizes Jenna is about to set her in Nick's lap. I don't blame her. Every adult she's been around has either been cruel to her, neglectful, or unable to do a damn thing to help her.

We've all let her down.

"Do you want to sit with her?" Nick asks.

I can't see Jenna's face but she's tense. She, like Cora, hasn't had the best luck with adults and here, a grown-ass man wants her to sit in his lap.

"I'm a little too big," Jenna murmurs.

"I'm strong." Nick winks at her, kindness in his smile.

With Cora in her arms, Jenna sits on his knee. Cora, now safe with Jenna, curiously reaches out to touch Nick's nose.

"Santa?" Cora whispers.

"Merry Christmas, Cora. You've been a good girl this year. I brought you some presents," he assures her.

"Sissy too?" Cora asks.

My heart cracks open. These two love each other. A bond forged from circumstance, but the love no less than if they had the same blood running through their veins.

"Sissy too," Nick says. "Both the best girls on my list."

Dane hands Nick their presents. First Cora's and then Jenna's. Cora likes all her gifts but fixates on the stuffed koala bear. I think Jenna might cry when she opens her Kindle. They eventually thank Santa and make their way over to me. Malachi ends up on Santa's lap next while I focus on Jenna.

Saddest fucking eyes, but she still seems so

strong. Despite everything. She needs a lifeline. I promised I'd give her one. It's Christmas after all. I don't think my decision over too long. I simply pluck the phone from my pocket and discreetly hand it to her. Her eyes widen for a moment as she registers what I'm giving her, and then quickly tucks it inside her hoodie pocket before anyone notices.

I did it.

I gave her a way to contact me, even though I could probably get fired for that move.

The guilt should overwhelm me, but all I feel is relief.

She won't drown.

I've thrown her a lifebuoy. I will save her. I will save them both.

"What's this?" I ask Cora as I point at her bear. "Is that a talking koala?"

She smiles bashfully at me as she offers me her stuffed animal. I take it from her and pretend to be the bear, making him yap to her about what *he* wants for Christmas.

"A new bike and a trampoline and a tree house," I say in a squeaky voice, wiggling him at her.

Cora giggles and the sound arrests my heart. So sweet and lovely. She's never warmed up to me, and I feel like I've crossed some huge barrier with her. When I look up at Jenna, she's staring at me with an odd look. I wink at her and her cheeks turn pink.

"I'm hungry," Joseph whimpers.

Barb glowers at him. "No snacks after supper."

I may have gotten them to take off the locks, but that doesn't mean I could make them take away their stupid rules. These poor kids should be eating ham and cookies and candy. It's Christmas Eve, for crying out loud. Not having to beg for a snack.

Nick's eyes gleam with fury and he opens his mouth, like he's about to say something, but I stop him with a shake of my head. We'll get them out of here. Maybe not today or tomorrow, but we'll get them moved once the judge has time to read over my reports. If we weren't right in the middle of the holidays, it'd move a lot quicker.

"It's time for Santa to go," Barb says in a cold tone. "He has other children to see." She walks over and plucks Xavier from Nick's lap.

"Thank you for allowing us to come," I grit out to Barb. My gaze flits over to Jenna once more as we head toward the door.

*Call me later when you can, and we'll talk.*

My unspoken message must reach her ears because Jenna nods. Her eyes glimmer with relief and I feel like I've done something right, no matter how unethical it is.

# six

*Jenna*

It's midnight after everyone has fallen asleep when I get the nerve to call Enzo. I've long put Cora to bed and she snores softly from across the room. My heart patters erratically in my chest as I mash his name—the only name—from the contact list. He answers on the first ring, as though he were waiting for my call.

"Jenna," he rumbles.

His voice, heavy with fatigue, seems deeper and scratchier. I can feel it clawing its way inside of me and making a home. It's far from an unwelcome feeling. In fact, my skin heats at my reaction to the way he says my name.

"Enzo."

He's silent for a beat. It makes me wonder if he's appreciating the sound of my voice too. Is he storing it away in his memory bank for later? Images of Enzo and I, together and not apart, flood my mind. Silly fantasies of myself and my new crush.

"How are you?" he asks, his voice finding its way back to polite and professional.

I'm slightly irritated that I'm over here fantasizing about him, and he's talking to me out of duty. "Fine," I clip out, sounding every bit like a bratty teenager. I wince because I want him to think of me as more.

"How are you really?" His chuckle warms me. It also warms me that he knows me better than to accept a dismissive reply to his questioning.

"Tired…"

"Well, it is midnight—"

"No," I interrupt. "I'm tired of everything."

"What does that mean?" he demands in a panicked tone.

My stomach flutters. "I'm not going to harm myself," I assure him. "I'm just tired of having to rely on people. I want to rely on myself."

"It's okay to need people."

Like him?

Why do I feel like lately, I need him? I need him to keep me safe from people like Juanita and Don. I need him to reassure me that everything's going to be okay, and that I won't drown. I need him to help me get the hell out of here.

"I need people," I concede. "Cora and…" *You*.

"Are you safe? Is your door locked?"

I stare in the dark at the door. It's closed, but the

door handle is gone. Don removed it after Enzo left earlier today.

"I'm safe." Lies. But what can he do about it? "What are you doing for Christmas?" I ask, desperate to change the subject.

"Going to Mom's," he says, a smile in his voice.

"Must be nice." I don't say it bitterly, just truthfully. One day, Cora will have the most wonderful Christmases. I'll make sure of it. I'll be eighteen in February, and then I'll change our lives for the better. So close.

"Jenna," he murmurs. "I know how you feel, and I'm sorry."

"Do you? Because I don't even know how I feel half the time," I grumble back.

"I was like you until..." He trails off and sighs. "Mom and Dad adopted me."

He was a foster kid too?

"Were you happy?" I breathe, tears swimming in my eyes as I try to imagine that day. A nice new mom and dad to come pick you up and give you the lovely life like in all the movies.

"I was. It came at a great cost, though," he says sadly. "Logan. They couldn't handle us both. They already had Elijah."

"I'm sorry," I whisper. If someone separated Cora and I, I'd lose my mind. Hell no. She's my baby. No one else's. Mine.

"I'm here if you need to talk, is all I'm saying."

Floorboards creak down the hallway and I freeze. "I have to go," I blurt out before hanging up. I hide the phone under my pillow and pretend to sleep.

*Creeeak.*

I crack open an eye, expecting to see one of the boys, but my skin grows cold at seeing Don. He stands in the middle of the room, wearing only his boxers.

*Go away. Go away. Go away.*

Instead of walking toward me, he makes his way over to where Cora sleeps. Panic stills my heart. When he reaches for her, I let out a sleepy groan, hoping to scare him away. He freezes and turns my way.

Clamping my eyes shut, I try desperately to calm my nerves. When I feel a warm hand on my cheek, I suck in a sharp breath. He moves his hand under the blanket and gropes my breast over my sleepshirt. I'm stunned, fear keeping me immobile, until he slides his hand further down. He gets as far as my lower stomach before I lose it. I claw at his arm and twist my body, kicking and flailing at him to get him away from me.

"Fuck!" he snarls.

My foot connects with his precious family jewels and he howls in agony, falling to the floor, gripping his bruised cock and balls. Cora starts to cry at having been woke up. I slip from the bed and rescue my baby while Don whimpers from the floor.

"Get out of my room, pervert," I hiss at him.

"Fucking bitch," he mumbles as he rises on wobbly legs, still holding his dick.

Cora buries her face against the side of my neck and twists my hair. I hold her to me, fighting off tears. The phone buzzes beneath my pillow several times. When she falls back asleep, I pull it out.

**Enzo: Are you okay?**

**Enzo: Jenna, let me know you're okay.**

**Enzo: If you don't answer, I'm going to call the police.**

I cry silent tears as I read his texts. Finally, I reply back to him.

**Me: I'm safe now, but I can't stay here much longer. Get me out of here.**

His response is immediate.

**Enzo: Do I need to come now?**

I turn the camera to me and Cora, and take a selfie that makes her jump from the bright flash. In the picture, she clings to me and I'm red-faced with tears soaking my cheeks. Most girls my age would be worried the guy they liked would see them at their worst.

I just want him to see me.

After I send him the picture, I type out a reply.

**Me: Tomorrow is Christmas. Enjoy yours. I can fight that bastard off until then.**

Before he can respond, I stow away the phone and fall asleep, praying that I truly can.

**Enzo: Merry Christmas!**

I groan as I squint at the morning light peeking in the window. It's an overcast day because it's snowing. Bright and obnoxious snow.

**Me: Bah humbug.**

He sends me a bunch of candy cane emojis and Santa faces, and I roll my eyes. Too early for this cheerful nonsense.

**Me: Go away.**

My phone that's on silent flashes with an incoming call.

"What?" I grumble.

He chuckles. "You're grouchy in the mornings."

"Spoiler alert: I'm grouchy in the afternoons and evenings too."

"Phone?" Cora asks, her sleepy eyes questioning me.

"Yes, phone. Shhh, our secret." I smile at her and kiss her forehead. "Want to talk to Enzo?"

"Kwala bear," she says, grinning.

"Your koala bear is right here," I tell her, handing her the stuffed toy.

"I have one better," Enzo rumbles. "Put me on FaceTime."

It takes me a minute to figure it out, and then we're staring at his handsome face. I hate that I probably look like a horror show right now, but it's worth seeing him in his festive red sweater.

"This," he tells us as he pulls a black cat into his lap, "is Halo."

"Halo? Strange name," I blurt out as Cora shrieks, "Kitty!"

He tilts the cat so we can see the white circle on the crown of its head. "For an angelic kitty, he's quite a little demon." He grins as he scratches the cat behind the ears. "Isn't that right, Halo? A little baddie with the mean ol' claws?"

Halo, unruffled by his teasing, cocks his head to the side and stares at us before letting out an unimpressed "meow."

Cora grabs the phone and tries to kiss it, effectively melting my heart in the process.

"My baby loves animals," I tell Enzo. "Right, banshee baby?"

Cora smooches the screen and giggles. "Cora lub kitty and Mommy and Zo."

My cheeks heat at her words. Enzo's smile falls and his brows scrunch in confusion.

"What time do you have to be at the festivities?" I ask, careful not to say any trigger words like "mom" around Cora.

"Noon. What are the plans there?"

There are no plans in hell. I keep this to myself because Cora likes to parrot the bad things I say.

"Just cuddle time, huh, Cora?"

Cora snuggles at my side. "Go bye-bye with Zo."

Enzo's eyes flash with pain as he realizes what Cora wants. "Hey, koala girl," he coos. "I'll come get you soon. Maybe tomorrow."

Both my brows lift in shock. "Tomorrow?"

He smiles. "If all goes in our favor, it could be as early as tomorrow. No matter what, I'm getting you guys out of there. Tomorrow, if we get a good judge."

The door gets pushed open, and I breathe a sigh of relief to see it's Malachi, followed by the other two boys.

"The monsters are calling us down to breakfast," Malachi grumbles.

"Yeah, the monsters," Xavier croaks in his frog voice.

Joseph cocks his head to the side. "Santa brought you a phone?"

"I gotta go," I tell Enzo. "Keep me posted."

He frowns but nods. I hang up without saying bye.

"It was Mr. Tauber. He's going to try to get us out of here tomorrow," I tell them, unable to hide my excitement.

The boys all rush forward, and the five of us hug in a disorganized way that still feels uplifting on Christmas morning.

"They can't know about the phone, okay?" I say,

patting them each on the head. "It's our secret. I can't tell on the monsters without it. If the monsters know, they'll take it away."

All the kids, including Cora, nod solemnly. We were all forced to grow up early. They understand what I mean.

"Last one downstairs is a rotten egg!"

# seven

*Enzo*

"Patty and Junior Grayson are good people," I assure Jenna as we drive.

Her brows are furled and she picks
at a string on her coat. "Right. If they were so good,
they'd have let the boys come too."

I let out a frustrated sigh. The Graysons only
had room for two more. Seth took the three boys and
placed them with another equally good home. When
Judge Rowe ruled in our favor this morning, I'd been
elated to pull all five from the Friedman couple, even
if it meant splitting them up. As long as Cora and
Jenna didn't get split, I considered it a success.

"I'm doing the best that I can, Jenna."

She looks over her shoulder and blows Cora a
kiss before turning to me. "I know," she admits, her
voice small and vulnerable. "I just always have to keep
my guard up."

I understand.

Hope for kids like her and Cora and the boys is useless.

It sure as hell was useless when I was a kid.

"Did you guys eat dinner?"

She snorts. "What do you think? That Douchebag Don would cook us a farewell meal? Right. You're a dreamer, Enzo." Despite her cynical words, she's smiling.

I'm supposed to take them straight over to the Graysons', but they need to eat. I turn off at the next exit before heading down to a diner that serves just about everything. When I park, Jenna flashes me a thankful smile that has my heart expanding. The girl could use to smile a little more often.

"Eat! Eat!" Cora cries out happily from the backseat.

I chuckle as I climb out of the car and unbuckle Cora from her seat. Surprisingly, she reaches for me. Not one to miss an opportunity, I pick her up and hold her to me. Cute as hell, this kid.

"You hungry, squirt?"

She grins at me. "And Mommy too."

I frown and look over at Jenna in confusion. Her face burns bright red.

"Sissy," she corrects Cora. "I bet you want a grilled cheese sandwich, huh?"

"Then let's get the girl a sandwich," I say to them both, smiling.

Jenna holds out her hands for Cora, but Cora rests her head on my shoulder.

"It's fine," I assure Jenna. "I've got her."

Jenna's green eyes narrow and her lips purse. When she's in Mama Bear mode, she doesn't seem like an almost eighteen-year-old girl. She seems like a grown-ass woman who's seen some shit in her life, and will do anything to protect her kid.

I pat the top of Jenna's head. "I've got this. Trust me."

Cora mimics me and pats Jenna's head too, earning a smile from our grumpy girl.

"Come on," Jenna says with a sigh. "I'm hungry."

We walk into the 1950s-themed restaurant and Cora squeals at seeing the train that zips along a track that is suspended from the ceiling. An Elvis song plays on the jukebox and we're greeted by a friendly white-haired waitress named Earlene.

She grabs a few menus and guides us over to a round booth in the corner. It's far too big for the three of us but we don't complain. Cora settles between Jenna and I. Earlene fusses over how adorable she is, and gives her some crayons and a coloring sheet before running off to grab some water for us.

"This is a fun place, huh, Cora?" Jenna says, smoothing down Cora's messy blonde hair.

"Train, Mommy," Cora chirps back. She stops coloring to point at the train that goes by.

"Mommy?" I lift a brow at Jenna.

"She gets confused sometimes," she replies, not making eye contact.

I let it go for now. I'll talk to her about it later when we don't have little ears listening. She corrected her the first time I heard it, but not now. In fact, everything she does encourages Cora's behavior toward Jenna.

Earlene returns to take our order. Jenna doesn't order much for her and Cora, so I add on a few extra sides for them to try, as well as my own order, including milkshakes. Both girls are all smiles when Earlene brings them fancy milkshakes piled high with whipped cream and topped with cherries.

"In February, I'll turn eighteen and we'll be able to have fun days like this all the time. Huh, Cora?" Jenna says to the toddler, her green eyes glittering with excitement.

Cora nods happily and babbles on about her koala bear. I'm still struck by Jenna's words.

"You'll have to get special permission to visit her," I remind Jenna.

"Visit her?" Her nostrils flare. "I'm not going to visit her, I'm going to adopt her."

The milkshake sours in my stomach. "Jenna, you know it doesn't work like that."

Green eyes bore into me, fierce and challenging. "Like what? A kid needs adopting. An adult wants to adopt them. They love each other. What more do they want?"

Proof of residence. Work history. Steady income. They certainly don't let just-turned adults adopt toddlers. It just doesn't work that way.

Earlene interrupts our tense moment by dropping off some mozzarella cheese sticks and some fried pickles. Jenna scowls as she eats.

"I'm just saying—" I start, but get cut off.

"Well, don't," she says bitterly.

We spend the next half hour eating in silence. Cora chatters happily and colors, but Jenna refuses to make eye contact with me.

"Go potty," Cora whines to Jenna.

They leave and I let out a frustrated sigh. If only love was enough, then a lot of kids would have better places to live. But love doesn't pay bills. Jenna has this impossible goal of adopting Cora and of course, I have to be the bad guy and pop her bubble.

By the time they return, I've settled the check and am waiting at the door with their coats. Jenna has once again shut down on me. At least Cora seems to warm to me with each visit. The drive to the Graysons' isn't far and when we arrive, both girls have lost their fire. Jenna's brows are scrunched together with worry, and Cora is shyly hiding in Jenna's hair. I scrub my face with my palm and guide them to the front door. A girl, probably around thirteen or so, answers the door.

"Unless you're selling Girl Scout cookies, we don't want any," the girl sasses in greeting.

I let out a chuckle. "I'm here to see Mr. and Mrs. Grayson."

The girl eyeballs me and then lets out a huff. "Miss Patty, you got more kids!"

"Well, let 'em in, Delia," Patty hollers. "They're gonna catch cold with you interrogatin' them like that!"

Jenna shoots me a panicked look.

I give her a reassuring smile. If my mom ever taught me anything, it's that some people are yellers but it doesn't make them mean. Some of the loudest people are as good as gold.

"Come on," Delia says, waving us in. "You came just in time to watch Faye burn the cupcakes. She burns everything."

"Cupcake?" Cora asks, perking up.

We follow Delia into the living room where Patty Grayson sits in a recliner. *Moana* plays on the television, and a little girl no older than five sits in the floor, playing with dolls. Another girl, maybe seven or so, is clipping bows into Patty's wild mane of orangey-red hair.

"Look what the cat dragged in!" Patty says with a snort. "Come on into the zoo. Always room for a few more monkeys."

Jenna stiffens from beside me. I gently pat her

back to let her know it's okay.

"Mrs. Grayson, this is Jenna, and the little one here is Cora. They'll be staying here," I say in greeting. "Girls, this is Mrs. Grayson."

A teenage girl bursts from the kitchen, frantically waving her hands in the air. "They burned, Miss Patty! I watched them. It said take them out between eleven and thirteen minutes. It's only been ten and they burned!"

Delia cackles. "Told you," she says to me and Jenna.

"When Junior gets home from work, tell him all about it. You know I've been tryin' to get that boy to give in and buy me a new oven. He never listens to me, but he can't ever tell y'all no." Patty picks up her glass of iced tea and takes a sip. "There's another box of that cake mix in the pantry. Just try it again and watch it, Faye. I'll pick some more up at the store next time."

Faye grumbles, but nods as she makes her way back to the kitchen, seemingly unfazed by our arrival.

"Jenna," Patty says, "the cupcake burner is Faye. She's sixteen. A real sweetheart. That sassy one over there is Delia. I don't know where she gets that mouth from." She and Delia both cackle with laughter, like it's an inside joke. Then, Patty points to the little one. "Noelle is five and she loves dolls. I bet you'd have fun playing with her, Cora."

"Dolls," Cora says softly and points. She wiggles and Jenna sets her to her feet. Then, carefully, she makes her way over to the little girl.

"And the stylist here is Lola. Lola is almost eight. A talented kid to be able to make this mess look nice," Patty says, waving at her hair.

I can't help but chuckle. She looks ridiculous with bows all in her hair, but Lola seems happy to play dress up with her. "Very talented indeed."

"Delia, hon, why don't you go show Miss Jenna where she'll be staying," Patty suggests.

Delia waves for Jenna to follow. Jenna glances at Cora, but she's already playing dolls with Noelle.

"She'll be fine," Patty assures her, her voice soft for the first time.

Jenna lets out a shuddered breath but nods. I walk with her up the stairs behind Delia. Delia gives us a quick tour of the space, and then shows her to a bedroom at the end of the hall.

"This one is you and Faye. The oldest always get the best room," Delia grumbles, but she doesn't sound too angry. "That one there is where the littles stay."

"Which one is yours?" I ask Delia.

"Well, it was with Faye, but then Miss Patty asked me to move in with Noelle and Lola because she said you'd want to be close to Cora."

I let out a relieved breath. When Patty and I spoke earlier, after Judge Rowe made his decision, I told her about how close they were, and that I seriously doubted Jenna would let Cora out of her sight.

"That's nice of you, Delia," I say to her. "Right, Jenna?"

Jenna begrudgingly nods.

"If you need me, I'll be in my new room, trying to get the smell of burnt cupcakes out of my nose," Delia informs us, before bouncing out of the room.

Jenna looks around the area and drops her bag to the floor. "They have a lot of stuff."

I bite back a smile. All the other houses were sparse in the bedrooms. This bedroom looks quite lived-in, from the colorful bedspreads to the white Christmas lights strung along the walls. Posters line the walls—some Asian boyband and Thor. Polaroid pictures, hundreds of them, have been stapled to the wall in a giant collage.

"They seem happy," I say gently.

I expect another bitter remark, but when our eyes meet, hers are glassy with tears. When her bottom lip wobbles, I can't help but go to her, and wrap her in a comforting hug.

"It's okay," I assure her. "Everything is going to be okay."

"I'm just so tired," she murmurs against my chest.

I stroke my fingers through her hair. "I know. I think you can rest now. This place is safe."

Her body relaxes against mine. "But what about her husband?"

Anxiety bleeds into her words. She tilts her head up to search my face for reassurance. With her green eyes wet with tears, they seem like glittering garnets.

"You text me later, or call me. Let me know the vibe. Remember, I'm here to protect you."

"I'm sorry about earlier," she blurts out. "I'm a mess lately. My emotions are all over the place."

"Understandably so."

She reaches up and gently cups my cheek. Her touch seems to electrify me, and I'm stunned by the sudden jolt of awareness that skitters through me. The sadness has melted away and her features are curious. I'm frozen in her gaze, unnerved by the change of our embrace. The moment went from comforting to something else.

"Jenna…" I start, my voice a husky rasp.

She bites on her plump bottom lip and frowns. "You smell good."

I can't help but smirk. "Thanks. You smell good too," I tease back.

I'm rewarded with an eye roll before she rests her cheek on my chest again. Comforting her feels like second nature. I inhale her hair.

"Smells like fried pickles," I inform her.

She giggles, the sound echoing around in my heart. "Gross."

"Not gross," I mutter before kissing the top of her head.

Her arms tighten around me. I wish I could just hold her forever. Jenna needs someone to hold her and remind her she's a great girl with a bright life ahead of her. Her childhood may have been shitty, but she's about to move on to a better stage in her life.

"If there's a way, will you help me find it?" she asks softly. Her head tilts up again.

I stay locked in her intense stare for a moment before I admire how pretty her features are. Simple, but classically beautiful. Perfect, pouty lips. The urge to kiss those lips has me pulling away from her. I give my head a slight shake to chase away thoughts that don't have any place around her.

"I'll look into it," I promise. "But you're going to have to do some legwork too, Jenna. A part-time job would be a great start. I can help you with that. Just let me know when you're ready."

"Thank you," she murmurs before stepping toward me and then standing on her toes. She plants a kiss on my cheek that sets my soul ablaze. "Thank you for helping me."

"I always will," I vow.

She rewards me with a breathtaking smile.

# eight

*Jenna*

*Three weeks later...*

I wake to the smell of something burning. Rubbing the sleep out of my eyes, I look over to discover Faye is missing, which means she's cooking. Faye cooking is always disastrous. I still can't help but smile. Patty and Junior are nice. Genuinely nice. I'd been worried when Junior showed up that first night. Waited for him to leer at me. But Junior was a big, overweight guy with nothing but eyes for his wife. Patty bosses him around, and Junior just does her bidding. Bought her that new oven she was after too.

I can hear Patty downstairs hollering but it no longer makes me flinch. She yells at everyone and is never mad. Ever. I've provoked her a few times to test her out and she simply changes the subject. As if I didn't let the word "bitch" slip out or refuse to load the dishwasher. After a few times of that, the guilt got a hold of me. Now, I try not to make trouble.

Cora's bed is empty, and I can hear her and Noelle squabbling over a doll in the room next door. Lola is playing peacemaker while Delia sings too loudly in the shower down the hall. It's truly not bad here. I don't mind riding the Patty and Junior Grayson wave until I turn eighteen in a little over a month.

My phone buzzes and I pull it out from beneath my pillow.

**Enzo: I thought I'd take you by the women's home today. Show you around where you'll be staying and let you meet the ladies there. You free?**

I groan as I reply.

**Me: Plenty of other things more exciting to do than that…like count the hairs on my head or listen to Lola play the clarinet.**

He shoots out a response before I even have a chance to sit up.

**Enzo: You need to do this. Besides, I thought I could convince you with some chips and queso. I know the key to your heart is food.**

I take an early morning selfie with my tongue sticking out and send it back.

**Enzo: Fix that bedhead, Oscar, and I'll be there in a couple of hours.**

A smile tugs at my lips. He's taken to calling me Oscar. As in Oscar the Grouch from *Sesame Street*. It doesn't even annoy me because I know I can be a bear sometimes.

**Me: Fine, you win.**
**Enzo: I always do.**

"Can we skip the visit and just go straight to the Mexican restaurant?" I ask, my nerves getting the best of me.

"Nope."

I roll my eyes at him, making him laugh. His laughter sends a flutter of excitement dancing through me. As he drives, I stealthily watch him. Today, he's as handsome as ever in his black coat and messy dark-brown hair. His curls are becoming quite unruly the longer his hair gets, and he's sporting a five o'clock shadow. My fingers tingle to touch him again.

It's been nearly a month since I saw him last. We've spoken on the phone and texted, but this is the first time I've seen him since our hug. That hug was charged. The way he looked at me was intense, and I've been fueled by that moment ever since.

"Do you have a girlfriend?" I ask him.

"Nope."

"Why not?"

He snorts. "I don't have a lot of time to date."

"Because of your job?"

"It keeps me busy."

I frown as I consider his words. I spend most of

my days gushing over every word he sends me and remembering that moment he hugged me like I was his, but then he says or does something to remind me I'm a duty to him.

Bitterness roils in my stomach and I blink back tears.

"Hey." His voice is deep and gravelly. "What's wrong?"

Shrugging, I avoid his gaze by looking down at my hands. "Nothing."

"Liar, but nice try. Tell me." He reaches over and pats my hand. His heat sears into my skin from the contact.

"I'm just a job to you," I whisper, hating how weak I sound.

He's quiet and I catch his eyes. Confusion and something else seems to war within his gaze. "Jenna…"

I thread my fingers with his. "Yeah, Enzo?"

His gaze falls to our joined hands. "You're more than just a job to me." He squeezes my hand but doesn't let go.

My heart races happily as we drive toward the shelter. He doesn't let go of my hand. I like how strong he feels, even from something as simple as holding hands.

Our moment is eventually stolen from us when we pull into the parking lot. I'm forced to get out and face our task at hand.

"This is all a waste," I utter under my breath as he ushers me inside. "I plan on getting a job and my own place. Cora can't live here."

He frowns and his lips press into a firm line. I'm not given a response as he enters an office inside. The next hour, I'm guided around the shelter. It lacks privacy and some of the women seem…rough. I don't want to be with them. I don't like the laundry list of rules the lady named Kim rattled out. It's kind of like a prison. As if being a foster kid hasn't been my prison already. It's like going from county jail to the penitentiary.

"What do you think?" Enzo asks, when we're back in the car.

"I don't think anything." Nothing good, at least.

"It's a good start," he assures me. "A good stepping stone before you're off and running into the real world."

"I guess," I utter.

He's quiet for the rest of the drive. We end up in a hole-in-the-wall Mexican restaurant. It smells so good my stomach grumbles. They take us to a booth in the corner that's barely lit up by a dingy bulb.

"Some place you've taken me to," I joke, unable to keep the smile off my face. It may look like a shithole, but it smells heavenly.

"Best salsa in all the land." He grins at me from

over his menu. In this lighting and the mischievous look on his face, I can almost imagine he's my boyfriend and we're on a date. When my cheeks heat, I thank God for horrible lighting.

Moments later, they bring the chips and salsa, earning my agreement. I let out embarrassing sounds of delight as I inhale my food.

"What are your plans after graduation? College?" he asks.

"I figured I'd need to get a full-time job in order to take care of Cora. I'm not sure how I'll be able to do college and work," I admit.

His features darken. "Jenna…"

"I know, Enzo. You don't approve of my goals. My guidance counselor would be happy to agree with you. You two could have a party discussing what a stupid girl I am." Thoughts of Miss Bowden with her pretty blonde hair and perfect body make me groan.

"You're not stupid," he growls.

"I just have stupid ambitions."

His nostrils flare, anger flickering in his eyes. "They're not stupid, just unrealistic."

"I have to try," I tell him, my voice cracking with emotion. "I have to try to keep her because she's mine. No matter what the stupid law says, or my age or the fact we're not blood-related, she's mine. I will fight for her. I'll do whatever needs to be done. I love her." Thoughts of leaving her in a little over a month has tears leaking from my eyes and snaking down my cheeks.

"Hey," he rumbles as he vacates his side of the booth to slide into mine. I'm pulled into his warm embrace. He holds me while I release some of the pent-up anxiety inside me through a quick cry.

"She's worth any stress and any obstacle. I may not be her real mom, but I'm more of a mom than anyone has ever been to her," I tell him fiercely. Lifting my head, I meet his intense stare. "I wish I'd been worth it to my mom."

"You're worth it," he practically snarls. "Don't ever think otherwise."

His masculine scent is comforting and coupled with his closeness, I can't help but lean toward him. He doesn't move away. His hazel eyes burn into me as he watches my every move. I tentatively touch his scruffy cheek, and my lips press to his on their own accord. Soft and gentle. He seems stunned and doesn't move away. But then his strong hand slides into my hair. Our lips part in unison. The moment his tongue slides along mine, I let out a low moan of appreciation. He tastes like yummy salsa and Enzo, a perfect, addictive combination. His kiss goes quickly from sweet to domineering. I let him take control of the kiss I started. He kisses me like he has the power to chase away my demons and my sadness. I kiss him back like I'm holding him to it. Finally, he breaks away. Intensity blazes in his eyes as he runs his thumb along my still-wet cheek.

"We shouldn't have done that," he whispers, his lips a hair from mine.

"But we did, and it was good."

A smile tugs at his lips but he pulls away, almost reluctantly. My heart is skittering along inside my chest. Happiness seems to buzz through my every nerve ending.

"We can't do it again," he says in a gruff tone. "No matter how good it was."

Before I can demand to know why not, the server brings our meal. Enzo stays on my side of the booth, which I consider a small victory.

He played it safe through dinner and I hated how he seemed to distance himself from me. When we make it to the car in the dark parking lot, I confront him.

"You can't hide from it," I bite out. "From this thing that's brewing."

He scowls as he starts for his car door. "Nothing is brewing."

Stepping in front of him, I block him from getting in the car. "*We* are brewing. You can't lie to me and tell me you don't feel it. If you didn't, you wouldn't have kissed me in there. You wouldn't want to do it again."

His brows deepen as anger flickers in his eyes. "We don't always get what we want, sweetheart. You, of all people, know this."

"But we could," I tell him, touching his jaw with my fingers.

"You're a child, Jenna. It's fucked up."

My face heats at his words. "I am *not* a child."

"You're not legal, so that makes you a child." His voice comes out like a sneer.

Fury bubbles up inside of me. I slap his cheek with a soft pop, making us both flinch in shock.

"I grew up a long time ago. I am that girl's mother. You and I both know it," I tell him, fire in my words. "Don't you dare insult me again, Lorenzo Tauber. If you're not attracted to me, then say it. If the kiss sucked, then say it. But don't tell me I'm a child."

His jaw clenches as he glares at me. Then, he steps toward me, palms cradling my cheeks. "I'm attracted to you. The kiss was everything. I'm sorry."

I let out a sigh of pleasure when his lips crash to mine. His body, hot and strong, presses mine against the side of his car as he kisses me. I let out a moan when I realize how hard he is in his jeans. Our kiss grows more heated, our hands more urgent. My palms slide up under his shirt and I touch the hard muscles on his lower back. This makes him growl as his hands grip my ass. I'm lifted and my legs wrap around his waist. The moment he grinds against my center, I moan into his mouth. My head falls back in pleasure, yanking us from our kiss.

"Jenna…fuck," he curses. His lips don't leave my flesh, though. He peppers kisses along my jaw to my ear. When he nips at the lobe, I gasp. "This really can't happen." He licks my neck and then bites the skin there. "Maybe in another month or two, but not right now."

"But we both want it."

His mouth is back on mine, kissing me in a re-assuring way. "Hell yes, we want it, but I need to get you back home. You're still my… I can't do this while I'm responsible for you." He pulls back and rests his forehead on mine.

I groan when he releases me and helps me back to my feet. "I was having the best night of my life until you ruined it, you know."

He grins at me, boyish and playful. "Best night of my life too, sweetheart. We have plenty more ahead of us. Can you be patient for me?"

He hasn't let me down yet.

What's another month of waiting?

I've waited my entire life for something good, and finally, something is within my reach.

# nine

*Enzo*

*One month later...*

"She's sick again," Jenna tells me, her voice taut with worry.

I glance over at the clock. It's late, nearly one in the morning. "Her ears?"

"Yeah," she says tearfully. "She's so hot and I can't rouse her."

"That doesn't sound good. Go and wake up Patty, sweetheart."

"Okay, I will. Enzo?"

"Yeah?"

"I'm scared." Her voice wobbles and my chest aches for her.

"I know. Go get Patty and keep me posted."

As soon as we hang up, I throw on some clothes and brush my teeth. This goes beyond my duties as a caseworker, but I don't care. Jenna needs my support. She's going to need it a helluva lot more when she has to leave Cora and go out on her own.

The thought is a dark one that unsettles me.

When we talk on the phone, she's just sure she can make it work. I'm the realist though, and know better. Unfortunately, I don't have the heart to tell her how wrong she is anymore.

**Jenna: We're headed to the hospital.**

I throw on some shoes, grab my coat, and I'm out the door within five minutes. It's cold as hell this February night, but at least traffic is nonexistent. I arrive at the hospital ten minutes later, just as Patty and the girls pull up. Climbing out of my car, I stalk over to them, my nerves brittle with worry.

"Mr. Tauber," Patty says, frowning. "Didn't expect to see you here."

"I called him," Jenna tells her as she unbuckles Cora from her seat. "I wasn't sure if you had all her medical information."

Patty nods, still seemingly confused as to why I'm here.

"Here," I say to Jenna. "Let me get her."

She steps out of the way and I pull Cora into my arms. The poor girl is limp and hot as fuck. I smooth her hair down and kiss her head. With my free arm, I hug Jenna to my side.

"It's going to be okay," I assure her. "They'll get her fixed right up."

Jenna gives me a watery smile and nods before

pulling away. While Patty sets to checking Cora in, I sit with Jenna in the waiting room. She leans her head on my shoulder. With both girls with me, something feels right and whole in my world. An ache that seems ever-present seems to disappear.

"How are you holding up?" I ask Jenna.

Her hand slides into mine and I give it a squeeze. "Better now."

Cora stirs and whimpers, which makes Jenna nearly break the bones in my hand with her death grip.

"Shhh," I say to them both. "It's okay."

Cora goes back to sleep and Jenna relaxes.

"What did you think about those job postings I sent you?" I ask, hoping to distract Jenna from her stress.

"The filing clerk job at the law firm sounds kind of boring," she says with a sigh. "But the receptionist job sounds good. They have good hours too, which would be nice for Cora."

I bite my tongue so I don't say anything about her Cora comment. "My friend Drew owns the physical therapy clinic. I know it's only a receptionist job, but he takes on a lot of interns. You'd mentioned you were interested in getting into medicine one day. Might be a good place to have your foot in the door, especially while you go to college. I can put in a good word."

"Okay."

A relieved sigh rushes past my lips. "Okay. Tomorrow, fill out that application, and I'll text him to let him know it's coming."

"Thank you, Enzo. I'll do whatever it takes for her."

I squeeze Cora as I try to play off my wince. Jenna thinks she can get a job and then adopt Cora. God, if only it were that simple.

Eventually, Patty joins us and we wait forever until they call us back. The nurse takes her vitals, runs some tests, and then rushes off to get the doctor. Moments later, a dark-haired guy in his mid-forties pushes past the curtain into our room.

"Looks like we have a sick little girl here," the doctor says in greeting. "I'm Dr. Venable." His green eyes are intense and familiar, but I can't place that I know him.

"I think it's her ears," Jenna says. "Frequent ear infections."

Dr. Venable jolts at her words and whips his head in her direction, as if only noticing her for the first time. "Gayla?"

Jenna frowns. "Jenna."

I stiffen and sit up in my chair, exchanging a look with Patty. Neither of us seems to like the way he looks at Jenna. "Is there a problem?"

Dr. Venable stares at Jenna for a beat longer and then gives me a slight shake of his head before turning back to Cora. He spends some time listening to her lungs, looking in her ears and throat, and checking her over. The room becomes awkwardly quiet. This ER doctor has no bedside manner whatsoever.

"Double ear infection. I'm going to check on her strep test that Nurse Becky administered. She's dehydrated, so I want to start her on some fluids. We'll get her something to take her fever down too. Hang tight," he says, before slipping from the room.

Patty unzips her purse and starts digging around. "Was it just me or was Dr. Creepy being weird?"

I snort out a laugh. "He was definitely weird."

Nurse Becky comes back and it takes all four of us to hold down a screaming Cora for her to get the IV needle in. Jenna ends up crawling into the bed and holding her before Cora calms down. They fall asleep in each other's arms. Soon, Patty falls asleep in her chair, snoring so loud I'm tempted to kick her chair to wake her up. I'm tired myself, but I can't stop looking at them.

Jenna and Cora.

A pair brought together by fate.

Two girls who will soon be separated.

Jenna's birthday is looming in a week. When she turns eighteen, both their worlds are going to be tipped upside down.

"You her husband?" Dr. Venable asks quietly when he peeks in to check on things.

My heart does a possessive thump in my chest. I push away those thoughts and shake my head. "Her caseworker. Why?"

I don't like his interest in Jenna. It unnerves me.

"She looks like someone I used to know," he mutters.

"You don't know her," I clip out. "She's seventeen. A foster kid."

His green eyes lock with mine. It's then I start to realize where the familiarity lies. They remind me of…

"Seventeen, huh?" He squeezes his eyes shut and pinches the bridge of his nose. "Does she know who her father is?"

I tense and narrow my eyes at him. He's tall and fit. A young doctor with a handsome face. When his eyes grow stormy and tortured, my gut hollows out because I've seen that expression before on someone else. Fuck. "No, she doesn't."

He runs his fingers through his hair. "This is going to sound really crazy, but…" He sighs. "I heard her voice. It sounded just like a woman I saw back when I was in medical school. School was stressful and she helped take my mind off things. And then, when I saw her…"

I glance over at Jenna as she sleeps. So beautiful and serene.

"She is a spitting image of Gayla," he says gruffly.

"I don't know what the protocol is, but I'd like to see if she's…" He trails off, like he can't bring himself to finish.

I snap my attention to him. This is the last thing she needs right now. False hope or a new daddy. Either way, it'll fuck with her already fragile state of mind. "Give me your number and we'll see about it later."

"Or we could see about it now," a voice says from the bed.

Jenna is watching me with her glimmering green eyes.

"You think you might be my father?" she asks Dr. Venable.

He steps into the room and nods. "Gayla and I were careless back then. The stress was overwhelming. At one point, I wondered if maybe she was pregnant. But then she ghosted me. Left without so much as a goodbye. I never saw or heard from her again. I'd even looked her up throughout the years, until…" He trails off and looks down at his feet.

"Until what?" Jenna asks softly.

"I'd learned that she'd died. Took her own life."

"There are procedures and protocol we have to follow," I utter tiredly at them.

"Do the test," Jenna tells him. "Take blood or whatever you need."

He slips from the room and is gone without

another word.

"Jenna," I groan. "For something like this, I'm going to have to file paperwork."

"I'll be eighteen by the end of the week. I'll do the test, Enzo. This is my life we're talking about." She strokes her fingers through Cora's hair. "Her temperature has gone down."

I stand and walk over to the bed. Taking Jenna's hand, I give it a squeeze. "People look alike. Don't get your hopes up." *About this. About Cora. Hope is dangerous to a person in the system. Hope most assuredly lets you down.*

"I'd rather rule it out and move on with my life," she says. "But if he's my father…" Tears brim in her eyes and she swallows. "I'd want to know my family, if there was a chance. You, of all people, should understand that."

Mom and Dad and Eli are my family, but if there was a chance to know my real mother and father, I'd jump on it in a heartbeat. Everyone wants to know where they come from. If they have other siblings or health issues that could be passed down. Knowing gives you a power you're not granted when you're an orphan.

"If that's what you want, I won't stop you." I let out a defeated sigh. "I just don't know about it."

She smiles in a conspiratorial way. "You were never here."

Dr. Venable comes back with a nurse. The nurse is curious now, after whatever Dr. Venable said to her, because she keeps studying Jenna.

"Daniel," Dr. Venable says, offering his hand to Jenna. "My name is Daniel. Thank you for wanting to do this."

The nurse winks at Jenna and then sets to swabbing her inside cheek first. After she encloses the swab in a labeled case, she does the same for Daniel.

"Typically, it can take a couple of weeks," Daniel explains. "But I am having it sent to a private lab. It'll cost a bit extra to have it expedited, but they can get us results in a couple of days." As soon as the nurse leaves, he switches back to doctor mode. "As far as this little one goes, it's not strep. I'd recommend after the antibiotics have set her straight to get some tubes put in her ears. I know a great ENT specialist."

Patty snores so loud she wakes herself up. She sits up, her wild eyes darting all around as she tries to pat down her mess of orange-red hair. "What'd I miss?"

"Cora needs tubes, like I've been telling everyone, but she's going to be okay," Jenna says, relief in her eyes.

"I'll have a nurse call the ENT specialist to get that scheduled," Daniel assures her. Then, to me, he says, "And here's my card. In case you need me."

I pull one of mine from my wallet. He'll need to get a hold of me when they get the results of the test. "We'll be in touch."

# ten

*Jenna*

*Three days later…*

I try to focus on Coach Long's lecture, but Winter keeps making faces at me. Each time, it takes effort not to giggle. I like Winter. She's different than all the girls at this school. Older and more mature acting. Usually. Right now, she's acting like she's twelve, but apparently that's exactly what I need. My phone buzzes with a text from her.

**Winter: Why the LONG face?**

I smirk and dart my gaze to Coach to make sure he doesn't bust me for not paying attention.

**Me: Ha. You're so punny. Just stressed.**

**Winter: Duh. You have bags under your eyes and you're twitchy. What's up?**

I frown about the bags comment, but I know it's true. I haven't been sleeping much lately.

**Me: You don't want to know.**

**Winter: I do…otherwise I wouldn't ask. Don't**

be so difficult. Spill.

**Me: It's complicated.**

She snorts, causing Coach to swivel around and glare at the class. Everyone sits a little straighter until he turns back around.

**Winter: You're so grumpy and secretive. Lucky for you, I have the patience of a saint. Now tell me what the hell is wrong with you before I get us both sent to detention where I can spend an hour bugging it out of you.**

I curl my lip at her and discreetly flip her off.

**Me: Oh, let's see. In a couple of days, I turn eighteen. They'll send me to live with a bunch of women I don't know. I'll have to leave my little girl. I'm starting a new job soon so I can try and have a work history so I can adopt her. And her doctor might be my dad, pending a paternity test. Also, I want to bang my caseworker. I bet you wish you'd never asked.**

When I look up, her eyes are wide as she types back.

**Winter: No, asshole, you're the most interesting person I've ever met. You have a kid? And OMG, you want to fuck your caseworker?!**

**Me: She's not mine by blood but she's mine. And he's so hot.**

**Winter: Want to go get coffee after school? You can tell me all about your girl and the hottie. My treat.**

My chest tightens. Winter is trying to be my friend. I don't make many of those. The only people I'm remotely close to besides Enzo and Cora are Patty and Faye. Having a friend seems like a luxury I can't afford.

**Me: I should get home to Cora.**

**Winter: I'm sure Cora will be fine for half an hour. Want to check first and let me know?**

Winter walks into the coffee shop, turning the heads of everyone in the process. She's beautiful. Curvy and bright and sexy. The girl has boobs for days. Meanwhile, I feel like a skinny, boring, beanpole in comparison. When she sees me, her bright red lips curl up into a smile. I can't help but smile back at her.

She orders our coffees and then makes her way over to me.

"Wow," she says as she settles into the chair across from me, passing me one of the cups. "You should smile a little more often. I didn't know you even could."

I stick my tongue out at her. "Brat."

"There's the girl I fell in love with," she teases. "Cora okay?"

"Yeah, Patty says she's fine. They're making dumplings for dinner." I smile tightly. It makes me happy she's having fun, and that Patty is a good person to all us girls, but I'm slightly jealous too.

"You don't seem happy about that," she says, studying me.

"I don't know…" I trail off and sigh. "It's weird. For her whole life, it's been me she has counted on and needed. I've been the only reliable person in her life. Now, with Patty and the girls, she has options." Tears burn at my eyes.

"Hey," Winter coos, grabbing my hand. "You're still her favorite."

A tear leaks out and I hastily swipe it away. "She calls me Mommy. I want to be her mom so bad, Winter."

Her brows furrow together. "It sounds like, to her, you already are her mom. People can have more than one person in their life. They can have friends." She squeezes my hand. "I tend to scare off all my friends because apparently sometimes I'm a cold bitch, but you're kind of frosty yourself. Ice queens need friends too."

I let out a chuckle, despite the tears now rolling down my cheeks. "How do people even put up with us?" My mind is on Enzo. He's always so in tune with my emotions. Seems to always say the right thing at the right time. Our late-night phone calls are something I've grown addicted to. Each night, he lets me vent about my frustrations.

"We're worth it, that's why," she says, grinning. "Now, tell me about the caseworker guy. What's he look like?"

I pull out my phone and find a selfie he sent me. A simple smiling one. "His name is Enzo."

"Older," she notes, and then makes a growling sound like a lion. "I approve. He's hot."

Laughing, I tuck my phone away in my hoodie pocket. "We kissed."

"You kissed your social worker?" she hisses. "I thought this was some unrequited love tale, but ol' boy wants you too. This just gets juicier and juicier."

"Things got hot and heavy, like, a month ago, but then he put a stop to it. He wants to wait until I turn eighteen, which I get. At least he didn't completely shut me out. We talk every night on the phone." I sigh happily. Enzo is the only constant in my life I can rely on. It's also the only selfish thing I do for myself. Everything else is for Cora. My stolen moments with Enzo are a gift.

"I can see where he'd worry about his job and, you know…other mundane stuff, like jail time." She laughs. "At least he's got a brain inside that pretty head. So, you turn eighteen and you've got a sexy man waiting for you. Can't see why that would have you crying."

"That's the good part," I admit. "I just don't know what I'll do about Cora. I want to adopt her, Winter.

She's mine."

Her brows furl together. "But it's not that simple, is it?"

Shaking my head, I pick up my cup of coffee that is starting to cool. "Enzo says they won't let me have her. But I'm starting a job next week at a physical therapy place. I'll get an apartment as soon as I can and get out of the women's shelter. I will do whatever it takes to provide for Cora."

"My boyfriend's an attorney. If you want, I'll ask him if he can help you," she offers with a smile.

"Really?" I shriek, earning a few startled stares nearby. "I'd be so thankful."

"No problem. Now, tell me about this daddy of yours," she urges. "You're like a walking Maury Povich show."

"Ha," I deadpan. "This doctor we met at the ER the other day was staring at me strangely, as though he recognized me. Then, he tells me that I look like a woman he dated. Next thing I knew, we were getting swabbed for a paternity test."

"What if he's a creep?" Her brows are furrowed in concern. "Sounds a little weird to see a girl and then demand a paternity test. What's weirder is you agreed. What does Hottie Caseworker think about all this?"

I sit up straight and frown. "He let me. Unofficially."

"Sounds sketchy. He's worried about fucking you

because you're underage, but he just stands by to let you take a paternity test? I'm no attorney yet, but everything about this feels fishy."

"It's not fishy," I defend, my cheeks burning hot. "If you'd seen the way Daniel had looked at me…"

Her brow arches as if she's waiting for an explanation. "And?"

"He just seemed so sure. Like he knew me."

"Listen," she says softly. "Don't get your hopes up. Could have just been some creep needing an excuse to stare at you. Probably goes home and whacks off to your innocent, grumpy face in his head."

"Gross," I grumble, fighting a smile. "If he's my dad, I don't know what I'll do."

"Just be careful," she says. "Promise me."

"I'll be careful."

"And promise me something else."

"I'll try."

"Let Enzo take you out for your birthday. For one night, don't worry about Doctor Daddy or little Cora or your job or your future. Go and do something for you."

"You know," I say with a smile, "you have a warm heart for an ice queen."

Her grin is wicked. "Yeah, well, don't tell anyone my secret."

"Your secret is safe with me."

"Yours are safe with me too."

"Hello?"

"Hey."

Enzo makes a manly groaning sound that sends ripples of excitement running through me.

"Did I wake you?" I murmur.

"No," he lies. He yawns, and I can't help but smile. "Are you in the closet?"

"Yep. Smells like Faye's feet too."

He chuckles, deep and gravelly. "Maybe you should go back to bed."

"I can't sleep."

"Is Cora okay?"

"Yeah," I say, my voice cracking with emotion. "I feel like time is ticking away."

Silence stretches out before us and then he speaks. "Your life is about to begin, sweetheart. You'll finally have control over it."

But I won't. I will still be grasping for things I'm not supposed to have.

"I don't want to leave her," I admit, tears threatening. "I can't, Enzo."

"Hey," he croons. "We'll figure it out. Just give me some time. She's safe with Patty in the meantime. You know this."

I do know this, but it doesn't make it any easier. Cora won't understand when I'm forced to leave in a couple of days.

"Friday, I'll come over to Patty's after school to pick you up. You can pack up and say goodbye to Cora for now. I thought maybe I could do something special for you for your birthday," he rumbles. "You don't have to check in until Saturday afternoon."

Despite all the uncertainty and stress, his words send a flutter of butterflies dancing through me. "Are you asking me out on a date, Enzo?" I smile in the dark closet.

"That, and much more. I'll take what I can get."

# eleven

*Enzo*

I stare down at my text in shock.

**Daniel: She's mine.**

He's attached a picture of the results and after I carefully study it, it's as clear as day. Daniel Venable is a perfect DNA match to Jenna.

**Me: Let me talk to her first. I'll let her know.**

His response is immediate.

**Daniel: Can I have her number? I would like to get to know my daughter.**

**Me: If she wants to talk to you, she'll call you. Jenna has had a hard life and is going through a difficult time right now. Pressuring her for a relationship right now isn't a good idea.**

**Daniel: Is it money? I can give her money if she needs it.**

**Me: Patience. Just give her some of that for now.**

**Daniel: I can do that. For now.**

With a sigh, I climb out of my car and head

toward Patty and Junior's front door. Delia answers before I have a chance to knock.

"Good luck," is all she utters before scampering off.

There's a loud commotion upstairs and I rush to the second floor. When I make it to Jenna and Cora's room, my heart sinks. Jenna sits on the bed, clinging to Cora and sobbing. Not just a few tears, but full-on hysterical crying. Cora is crying too, as they hold on tight to each other. Faye sits on the bed nearby with tears in her eyes as Patty hugs her.

Oh boy.

"They're saying their goodbyes," Patty says, her voice quivering with emotion. "Come on, Faye. Let's give them a moment."

They exit the room, leaving me with the two crying girls. I sit next to Jenna and pull them both in an embrace. Jenna seems to break apart in my arms. She melts against me.

"I-I c-can't l-leave her," she chokes out.

"You have to."

Cora starts crying harder and chanting, "No," over and over.

I pull away and run my fingers through Jenna's hair, gently tugging so she looks at me. "Listen, sweetheart. You have to be strong, okay? You have to be strong for her. You're not saying goodbye forever. Just bye for now. You cry, she cries. Understand?"

She squeezes her eyes shut and her face contorts into a heartbroken expression. Tears stream down her cheeks, but she nods. Her bottom lip trembles wildly. "I c-can d-do this."

"You can, and you will," I agree, smoothing out her hair.

I stroke Cora's hair and kiss the top of her head. "Cora bear, Jenna is going to go bye-bye with me, okay? You get to stay and help Miss Patty cook again. You like helping Miss Patty, right?"

Cora nods and looks up at me. "Cupcake."

"I bet Faye will want help with making cupcakes," I agree. "Can you be a big girl and tell Jenna you'll see her later?"

Cora moves to sit in my lap and then she pets Jenna's hair like I've been doing. "Make cupcake, Mommy?"

Jenna nods, more tears racing down her cheeks. "Make cupcakes and I'll come back to see you soon. Okay?"

"Okay," Cora agrees. "Kiss bye-bye."

"You better give me some kisses, banshee baby," Jenna says, tickling Cora and making her squeal. Then she sets to kissing all over her face as Cora cackles with laughter. "I love you, Cora."

"Love you, Mommy."

"Go play with Noelle," Jenna whispers. "I'll see you soon."

Cora slides from my lap and toddles out of the room. I waste no time pulling Jenna to me and hugging her.

"You're doing great," I assure her. "I'm so proud of you."

She cries for another half hour, clinging to my chest and soaking my shirt with her tears.

I'd planned to take her to dinner and a movie. Maybe even shopping. But she's so broken and tired, I opt to take her home instead. Patty sent us with some leftover birthday cake that we can eat later. When I pull into my garage, Jenna flashes me a smile of relief.

"I'm in no mood to go out," she says sadly.

"Not right now, but one day, you will be. I can wait. But what I can't wait for is my growling stomach. What do you say, birthday girl? You want chicken stir-fry or spaghetti? Those are my two specialties and admittedly two of the only things I know how to cook."

She laughs. "Hmm, with all those options, it's hard to decide. Surprise me."

Leaning forward, I press a kiss to her supple lips. "It's going to be the best birthday dinner ever, I promise."

We exit the car and I show her around my house. Her glum mood has dulled as she takes to cuddling

Halo. Halo, happy for someone other than me to give him affection, purrs and snuggles against her.

"I know you mentioned you don't have many things to wear. You're welcome to snoop around in my drawers. Take what you want. Get comfortable. I want you to relax, Jenna," I murmur, stroking her hair behind her ear. "You're wound so tight. It's your birthday. You owe it to yourself."

"I'll try," she promises.

I leave her to go get dinner started. Spaghetti is the best thing I know how to cook, so I set to boiling water and browning the meat. Eventually, she walks into the kitchen wearing my sweatpants and hoodie. When she stands beside me, I smile because she smells like me too.

"My clothes look good on you," I tell her.

She laughs. "Spoken like a true man."

I set the spoon down and turn to her. Her eyes are bloodshot and swollen from crying, but she's still beautiful. "You're doing great, Jenna."

Her smile falls and her nose turns pink as she fights more tears. "Trying not to drown."

"I won't let you drown," I vow, as I dip down to kiss her.

"Promise?"

"Promise."

I kiss her again, but this time, she parts her lips to invite me for more. Sliding my palm up the side of her neck, I run my finger along her jaw in a gentle way. Her fingers grip the front of my sweater and she pulls me closer. Our tongues are desperately seeking one another. I have to force myself away from her sweet mouth before I decide to ditch dinner and have dessert instead.

"Tease," she mutters, her voice husky with need.

"Believe me, I didn't want to stop." I wink at her and then continue cooking. She busies herself in the kitchen, hunting down plates and cups. Soon, we sit down to a home-cooked meal. Her mood has visibly improved as she chatters on about one of her new friends named Winter.

"She wants to be an attorney. Can you believe that?" she asks as she twists noodles around her fork. "I mean, I've seen her argue with Coach Long and she's quite good at it. But an attorney? Sounds so boring."

I chuckle. "You sound like my friend, Nick. Are you nervous about starting with Drew next week?"

She swallows a mouthful and then shrugs. "He was nice on the phone. Described everything I'd be doing and it didn't sound too difficult. I'm kind of looking forward to it. Too bad it'll only be part-time until after school ends."

"It's a good start. What about college?"

Her nose scrunches as she makes a face. "I've applied to some places, but I don't want to go far. You know…just in case."

Just in case she doesn't get Cora.

"One day at a time," I tell her. "That's all you can do."

"Until then," she says with a sigh, "don't drown."

As the movie plays, I sneak peeks at her. She fell asleep ten minutes into the movie and has been out ever since. It's nice having her at peace on my sofa. As she sleeps where no worries can plague her, I'm free to stare at her in privacy. Our moments until now have been few and far between. Now that her age doesn't stand in our way, I look forward to seeing where this goes. I don't date often because my schedule is a mess. So finding a nice girl, to have dinner and watch a movie with, is difficult. With Jenna, this all feels so comfortable and easy.

Her eyes flutter open and she catches me looking at her. A smile plays at her lips. "Hey, creeper."

I smirk. "Hey. Might want to wipe off that drool."

She snorts and swipes at the nonexistent drool. "Punk."

"Want to come a little closer and let me see if you got it all?"

"I didn't drool," she argues, but sits up to make her way to my end of the sofa. Her legs straddle my thighs and she rests her palms on my shoulders. "What do you see?"

*A beautiful, broken girl, so worthy of love and affection it makes my heart ache.*

I rake my fingers through her hair, but don't let go when I reach the ends. What I want to say to her stays stuck on my tongue. Gripping the bottom of her hair, I tug until her throat is exposed to me. I press my lips to her skin and then run my tongue along the flesh. "I see you missed a spot. Don't worry, I got it." I chuckle against her neck and she shivers.

"I think there's some here," she murmurs, running her thumb along the side of her neck to her ear.

I press kisses along the trail to her earlobe. When I nip her there, she groans. Her hips move, causing her to rub against me. My cock is awake and at attention. The urge to grab her hips and pull her to my dick is overwhelming, but I refrain. It's nice letting her set the pace. For now.

"Enzo," she breathes, her fingers tangling in my hair.

"Yes, sweetheart?"

"I need more."

I smile against her flesh. As much as I'd love to fuck her right here on this couch, I can wait until she's emotionally ready. But that doesn't mean we can't do other things.

Gripping the bottom of the hoodie, I inch it up

slowly. She pulls away to stare at me. Her hooded green eyes blaze with lust. When she bites on her bottom lip, I'm unable to keep the slow act up. I want to see her. All of her. I tug the hoodie away and toss it beside me. My eyes roam down her front. Her full breasts jiggle in her simple bra with every breath she takes.

"It's the only one I have," she says sadly, shame in her voice.

I snap my head up to frown at her. "I was admiring how hot your tits looked, not criticizing your bra." I reach up, and pull the cups down to expose her rosy pink nipples to me. They're erect and begging to be sucked on. "You know you never have to feel ashamed with me."

She nods and I lean forward to inhale her. Jenna always smells sweet, like sugar cookies or something. My mouth waters for a taste of her. I press a soft kiss to the delicate skin between her breasts. Innocent and gentle. But then I suckle on the curve of her breast, tonguing the warm flesh all the way to her nipple. When my wet mouth latches on to the pebbled nub, she cries out. I suck her nipple hard enough to make her jolt in my lap. Then, I tease away the pain until she's squirming and panting for more. On and on, I tease her nipples, alternating back and forth.

"Enzo," she murmurs, her hips rocking along my hard cock through our clothes.

"If you keep that up, I'm going to come in my pants," I growl in warning. "Sit up on your knees."

She unfastens her bra and tosses it away before heeding my words. My sweatpants she's wearing have been rolled down several times to fit her in the waist. I pull the front of them down, along with her panties, and dip my head down so I can peek at her cunt. Her hair is dark and trimmed neat. I want to bury my nose against her and memorize her scent.

"This," I rumble as I kiss her softly on her pubic bone, "is mine."

She gasps as my hot words tickle her flesh. A low moan rumbles from her the moment I flick my tongue out and taste her. Her pussy is soft and untouched. In our many phone calls, she'd confessed her virginity to me. As though it was something to be embarrassed about. I've jacked off more times than I can count to the thought of taking her virginity. Something sweet and delicate, and all mine for the taking. I want to own her pussy with my cock and tongue.

"Be a good girl and let me see what's hiding in there," I instruct, running my thumb along her slit. "Show me, sweetheart."

Her fair skin blushes at my words but then she reaches down to touch herself. My cock jumps in my pants at seeing her pull her pussy lips apart for me. Her clit, dark pink and perfect, seems to beckon for my tongue.

"Beautiful," I praise as I flick my tongue out and lap at the tiny bundle of nerves.

"Oh," she rasps in surprise, letting go of herself to clutch onto my hair.

I smile against her pussy and lick her again, this time firmer. I flatten my tongue against her clit and rub hard circles against it. Her breathing becomes strangled and the grip on my hair becomes nearly painful. But I don't dare stop kissing her perfect cunt. I massage it eagerly with my tongue, drinking up her sweet taste.

"Help me take these off," I instruct against her pussy, as I tug at her sweatpants.

She lifts a knee up and I slide the material down and off her leg. We do the same for the other leg. All that stands between me and my girl is a pair of pink panties.

"Tomorrow, I'm taking you to buy new undergarments," I warn as I rip right through the fabric.

"You just tore my panties!"

"Shh," I croon. "I'll make it better."

I grip her hips and flip us on the couch so I'm on my back. She stares down at me with confusion in her eyes. Her dark hair is messy and her tits look divine. I'm going to enjoy every second devouring this girl.

"I want you right here," I tell her, tapping my lips. "Hold on to the arm of the couch and let me do the rest."

She maneuvers her way to me and then settles her pussy on my face. I grip her hips as I get to sucking and licking on her pussy. Her arousal practically drips from her. I can certainly taste it. Sweet, like sugar. My palms slide to her ass and I squeeze her cheeks, pulling them apart.

"Enzo," she whimpers. "This is too much. It feels too…" Her body jolts and then she grinds against my mouth.

I suck and nip at her clit, knowing she's close. My fingers probe at her opening. She's slick and her body is needy. I push a finger inside of her, slowly, but don't stop until I'm as far as I can go. She whines at the intrusion.

"Fuck, sweetheart," I murmur. "Your pussy is so damn tight. I'm going to hurt you." Simple math tells me my cock is way too thick and long for her. Still, I want to try. Urging another finger inside her pussy beside my other one, I get to see just how tight she really is. Her channel grips my fingers, making me wonder if I'm hurting her. I push deeper inside her as I suck on her clit.

She hisses in pain that gives way to a moan. I fuck her gently with my two fingers, all while biting and sucking on her tender flesh. A shudder ripples through her and my name gets shouted from her lips. Her cunt clenches around my fingers in an unforgiving way as she rides out her orgasm. I suck on her clit, hard enough and long enough to send her into another orgasm that makes her seize violently. When I decide to give her a reprieve, I slide my fingers slowly out of her. A smear of blood is mixed with her arousal and guilt niggles at me.

"Did I hurt you?" I ask, my voice husky and raw.

"It stung, but it also felt good," she breathes. "Is that blood?"

I sit up and she settles at my waist, her legs spread as she straddles me. Her scent is addictive and nearly maddening. Going slow with her will be hard when every animal instinct in me is begging to roll her onto the floor and fuck her until she can't walk.

"You're not so innocent anymore," I tease, as I lick away the evidence on my fingers.

She bites on her bottom lip, her eyes glimmering with fascination. When I finish sucking away her sweet and now metallic taste, I slide my hand into her silky locks and pull her to my mouth for a kiss. Her soft moan tells me she likes tasting herself on me. The way she grinds on my cock an indicator she's ready for what comes next.

But she's not ready.

She's had a hard day and just needed the release I gave her. One day soon, I'll give her more. Just not today.

"Come on," I grunt. "Let's get ready for bed. You're tired."

"Bed?" Her nose scrunches in a way that indicates she doesn't agree. "I'm not tired, Enzo."

Ignoring her argument, I rise with her in my arms. Her feet slide to the floor. With her naked and in my arms, I can hardly think straight. My body begs to take her right now.

"What about you?" she murmurs, her small palm splaying on my lower stomach over my shirt.

A groan rumbles from me when she slides her hand down into my pants. She grips my cock and runs her thumb over the pre-cum on the tip. I stand helpless to her innocent seduction. I don't argue as she pushes my pants and boxers down my thighs.

"Like this?" she asks as she tugs on my cock.

I hiss out in pleasure. "Exactly like that."

She works my cock in her fist until we surprise us both when I come without warning. My seed splatters against her stomach. Before I can stop myself, I run my fingers through it and smear it all over her breasts. She watches wide-eyed at my work.

"I want to take you to bed and we can talk. One day soon, we can do more, but I want you to rest tonight," I explain, knowing she'll want reasoning as to why I can't fuck her on her eighteenth birthday. "Plus, I need to make sure you're okay with me. I'm not exactly a gentleman in bed, sweetheart. I leave bruises with my mouth. I like it rough."

She frowns at my words. "You want to hurt me?"

"Not in a way you won't enjoy," I assure her. "I want to fuck you against windows and force you to your knees to suck me off. I want to pull your hair when I'm fucking you from behind. And your ass…I want to push inside you and make you scream." My dick throbs back to life with an image of Jenna's ass prone and ready for me. "Which is why we should wait. I don't want you to be distracted by your emotions and do something you're not okay with. We can start small and gently."

"I want to do those things," she tells me bravely, lifting her chin. But her eyes flicker as though she's unsure.

"Then we'll work up to them. Come on. Bedtime, sweetheart."

# twelve

*Jenna*

I wake with a start, confused in the darkness. I'm sweating, and my hair sticks to my face and neck. A man is wrapped around me like I'm a human-sized teddy bear. My erratically beating heart slows as I stroke my fingers through his hair. Memories from last night drift to the forefront of my mind.

He made me come. Twice.

It was embarrassing to be so exposed to another person, but all shameful thoughts flew out the window when he licked and sucked and tasted me.

And his cock.

Oh. My. God.

I wish I could talk to Winter about it. I'm terrified of it, quite frankly. He's large. Really large. I have nothing to compare it to, but my hand seemed so small wrapped around it. The thought of him pushing in where he had his fingers mere hours ago is a terrifying thought. Will it hurt? Will we have sex before he sends me away to live at the women's shelter?

My gut hollows out.

After we wake up tomorrow, I'll have to ready myself to go to the shelter. It's childish to beg Enzo to let me stay with him, even if it is what I truly want. We've barely become intimate. I don't want to scare him away by clinging to him.

I let out a sigh. Tears sting my eyes as I listen for Cora's steady, soft snoring. It's absent, which feels like my heart is being smashed beneath a boot. I miss her. I'm going to miss her every second of every day until I find a way to get her back.

"What's wrong?" Enzo's husky voice makes me jolt in surprise.

"Nothing," I lie.

"You're crying in the dark, sweetheart." He pauses. "Is it me? What I said last night? You know I'd never pressure you into anything. If you want gentle, that's how I'll be."

I shake my head and tears roll down my temple. "I'm not afraid of that. I'm just hot."

The springs groan as he sits up. His shirt I'm wearing swallows me and is drenched in sweat. I breathe a sigh of relief when he pulls it away from my body and discards it. Now that I'm fully naked, a delightful shiver quakes down my spine.

"Better?"

"Much." A sob catches in my throat and the bed trembles as I try to contain it.

"Shh," he croons, pulling me against his bare chest. "I've got you."

"I miss her," I finally admit, giving in to the emotion threatening to drown me. "So much."

He rakes his fingers through my hair, untangling it along the way. "I know you do. She's doing fine, though. You know this."

"She belongs with me."

"I don't doubt that for a second."

"What if it takes too long?" I choke out. "What if she forgets about me?"

"She won't forget about you. No one could ever forget about you."

I lie there in silence as my tears dry and I cool off. Tentatively, I reach up and stroke my fingers along his chest. "I want you to…" I trail off, feeling stupid at my words. "I want you to make love to me like you would any other woman you were seeing. I don't want you to hold back if it's something you like. You said you wouldn't truly hurt me and I believe that." I tilt my head up, seeking his mouth. "I want you to distract me, Enzo."

His lips find mine in the dark and he kisses me desperately. As though I'm the air he's been gasping for. I moan when he rolls me onto my back and kisses a trail along my jaw to my neck. He nips my flesh hard enough to bruise. I zero in on the way my skin stings and now the way he tongues away the hurt. If this is the type of roughness he wants to use on me, I'll gladly be his victim. As he alternates between kissing and biting me, his hand trails south between my legs, where I'm already growing wet for him. I'm mesmerized at how easily he plays my body. How he knows exactly where to rub and touch to make me thrash in pleasure. He brings me over the edge, and I climax so hard I see stars in the dark.

He doesn't make a move, so I encourage him. It's easy to be brave in the dark.

"I need this," I whisper. "I want you to give this to me."

"At any time it's too much, tell me, sweetheart."

"I promise."

His mouth finds mine again and he dizzies me with a deep kiss. A tremor of unease skitters through me when he pushes my legs apart and settles himself between my thighs. His heavy cock rests against my pussy, but he doesn't do anything other than kiss me.

He's holding back.

Determination ignites within me. I don't want him to hold back with me. I want him to lose control. I want him to make love to me, like he has no other woman before. I want to be better than them. Digging my fingernails into his shoulders and my heels into his ass, I urge him to do what he wants to.

"I want you, Enzo. Take me away with you."

He grunts—feral and manly—before sliding his cock back and forth along my slit. The motion is teasing and it makes me crave more of him. His tip breaches my opening and it already stings. Slowly, achingly so, he dips in and out, inching deeper each time.

"Jesus, Jenna," he growls. "You feel so fucking good."

I melt under his praise. "You feel good too."

He pulls out slightly and then drives into me the rest of the way with one hard thrust. Our mouths clash together as he smothers my moan in a starved kiss. The pain between my legs gets ignored as I focus on the way he consumes me from the inside out. He's inside me. Making love to me. It feels as though we're linked now—linked in a way I've never been with anyone. Like he found a way to bind our souls together.

"Enzo," I rasp out. "Oh, God."

His hips thrust hard against me. The reverent way he cradles my cheek turns to something darker as his hand slides to my throat. He applies pressure and my pussy throbs in response. I'm gripped in his possessive hold as he drives into me over and over again. I like the way he holds me, as though I'll try and get away.

I'm not going anywhere.

My breaths are labored as he tightens his grip.

Instead of feeling panicked at my limited air supply, I feel more alive than ever. Electricity seems to buzz through my nerve endings, zapping all the erogenous zones. Pulses of pleasure throb in my core. He works his hips in such a way that he rubs against my clit about every other thrust. The movements make my legs shake with need. My fingers claw at his flesh, desperate to take that leap with him. I'm desperate for more—more of what, I don't know. I slide my hand over his. Permission. He understands my unspoken words and grips me tighter. His lips hover over mine in an almost kiss as he takes me over the edge of sanity. The room seems to spin as I lose control, climaxing hard.

"Fuck," he curses. His grip loosens as he jerks out of me suddenly. Heat splatters against my pussy that stings from the beating it just took. When he finishes, he leans forward to turn on the bedside lamp. He sits back on his haunches and stares down at me.

My first instinct is to close my legs, embarrassed at what he might see. But his hazel eyes darken as he roughly parts me back open.

"This," he murmurs, as he smears his cum with the palm of his hand against my pussy, "is beautiful."

I grin at him, feeling stupid and young, but also happy. Seeing this grown, gorgeous man admiring my body as though it's something wonderful can really help a girl's ego. "You're beautiful too."

And he is. Hard, sculpted abs. Broad shoulders. Dark hair between his pectoral muscles that matches the trail down to his cock that glistens from our cum. His dark-brown hair is tousled and messy in a way I've never seen.

He flashes me a cocky, playful grin before turning his attention back to my pussy. "Does it hurt?"

I shake my head. "Stings, but overall, it felt really good. I was scared it wasn't going to fit."

"I was too," he admits, his brows furrowing. "Did I hurt you anywhere else?" His gaze drifts to my neck.

"No," I mutter, my cheeks heating. "I really liked that part. I liked feeling you unravel and lose control."

He smirks. "I don't even recognize myself. I have zero control with you. It took every ounce of self-control I had to pull out. Are you on the pill?"

"No," I utter out, embarrassed. "I'm sorry."

His hand slaps my sore pussy and I shriek. "You're not to feel sorry about something like that, sweetheart. I'm sorry for taking you without asking. I'm clean, if you're worried."

"I know you'd never put my health in danger," I assure him.

He runs his knuckles along the inside of my thigh. Up and down. In a way that makes me want him to make love to me again. "I can take you to see your doctor. Buy you pills. In the meantime, we should use condoms."

"Okay."

His brows furl together. "Speaking of doctors…"

"What?"

"Come on. Let's shower and we'll talk."

He climbs off the bed and I stare after his muscled ass as he heads into the bathroom. My body aches all over but it's a good sort of ache. I can't wait to do it all over again with him. Sliding out of the bed, I can't help but smile. His cum is drying to my skin and it feels weird. A good weird. Like how an animal would mark his mate with his scent. I feel marked. Owned and protected. By the time I reach the bathroom, he's already started the shower and steam billows around. I follow him into the shower and stare up at him in question.

"What are we talking about?" I ask, pursing my lips together.

He frowns and settles his large hands on my hips. "Dr. Venable messaged me today."

The paternity results.

My heart threatens to jump right out of my chest.

"And?" I choke out.

"What do you want?"

I swallow, trying to imagine what having a father would be like. If he's not my father, I'll feel disappointed because I'll once again be all alone in this world, with no family. If he is…I can't let my hopes get up until I know for sure.

"I want to know either way," I tell him firmly.

"Daniel Venable is your father."

I blink at him in shock. Then, a wave of emotion washes over me. Tears well and spill down my cheeks as I allow myself to understand his words. I have a father.

"He wants to get to know you, but if you're unsure—"

"I want to get to know him too," I blurt out.

His smile is gentle and comforting. Like the social worker smile I've come to be so fond of. Despite being naked with my breasts smashed against his chest, his smile assures me, like all the other times before.

"He's asked for your number, so I'll give it to him now."

"Thank you," I choke out.

He pulls me close and kisses the top of my head. Then, he sets to washing my body while I stand there, motionless, my thoughts a never-ending blur. Enzo is just rinsing out my hair when I seem to come out of my fog. His touches no longer feel innocent as he lingers his fingers at my throat. Turning to face him, I launch myself at him. Our mouths crash together in the next instant. He grips my ass and lifts me before pushing me against the cold tile.

"Enzo," I plead.

"The condom," he groans. His cock throbs hard between us.

"Pull out again."

He doesn't have to be told twice. One second, he's rubbing his length against me and the next, he drives into me so hard I scream. Enzo, my always gentleman, has transformed into a beast who hungers to ravish me. I angle my head so my throat is prone to him. His teeth find the flesh and he bites me.

"Oh, God!" I cry out.

He slams into me so hard my head bounces off the tile, dizzying me. Watching Enzo lose control as he gets lost inside my body is the single most satisfying thing in the world. It makes me feel strong—as though I have some magical power. For always feeling weak my entire life, it's a breath of fresh air. His fingers tangle in my hair, his grip tight at the roots. The sting of my follicles pulling from my scalp as he forces my head up to look at him is thrilling. He nips at my bottom lip and I can't help but clench around his cock. From this angle, he drives deep inside me, bruising places I had no idea existed.

I love it.

I love him.

The thought is a terrifying one.

I've never been into anyone the way I'm into Enzo. The very idea of leaving him soon is nearly crippling. I want to stay wrapped up in his safe, protective arms forever.

"Sweetheart, I'm about to come," he growls.

"Touch your pretty clit and come with me."

Seduced by his raw words, I obey him. Our eyes lock as he fucks me while I finger my sensitive clit. It doesn't take long before my body tenses in anticipation. His name is on my lips as I dive into oblivion.

"Jenna," he groans, his cock throbbing. Heat stings at my insides, and then he's pulling out, shooting his orgasm out between us.

"We're playing with fire," he mutters huskily. "I was seconds from coming inside you."

I don't tell him that maybe he did come a little bit inside me. He seems so sure he didn't. I can't tell who he's trying to convince. I sure as hell am not convinced.

"What if you did?" I ask, chewing on my bottom lip.

His features darken. "Then you could get pregnant."

Neither of us says anymore on the matter. I'm not sure how he feels about that, but my heart does a tiny flutter. A little sibling for Cora to play with? I can't say the idea is one I hate. In fact, with Enzo, I want everything eventually. I just hope he wants it too.

# thirteen

*Enzo*

I sneak a peek at Jenna as we drive to the shelter. It fucking kills me to take her here in the first place, but what am I supposed to say? *I know we've just started fucking and I barely know you, but will you move in with me?* I cringe even imagining saying those words. If it were up to me, I'd tell her to screw the shelter and just move in with me. While we shopped together at the mall earlier today and then had lunch, we felt like a real couple. Better than any other relationship I've had in the past. With Jenna, it feels so natural. Like we belong together.

And that makes me feel like a creep for falling for her so quickly.

Since when do I fuck a girl and decide she's a keeper?

Not to mention how she must feel. I'm her first. But what if she doesn't want me to be her last?

If being a social worker has taught me anything,

it's that teen girls are wishy-washy and emotional. Especially girls who have lived their entire lives in the system. I've watched them act out one day and be good as gold the next. Jenna could wake up two weeks from now and wish she wasn't tied down to some man as old as her father. She might meet a physical therapist at Drew's and decide banging some guy closer to her age is more fun.

So, I bite my tongue.

The words are in my mouth, begging to be spilled.

*Stay with me instead.*

Jenna lifts her chin and stares out the windshield as we drive. She's brave and strong. I'll be damned if I take away her first taste of freedom because I want to keep her.

"Are you nervous?" I ask, my voice husky.

"A little."

*Stay with me instead.*

"I'm a phone call away," I tell her lamely. Fuck.

She gives me a small smile. It doesn't reach her eyes. "So is my dad."

I frown, unsure how to take that response. "Jenna…" *Stay with me instead.*

"My father wants me to stay with him instead of going to the shelter," she mutters. "But…"

"You want freedom."

She purses her lips. "I don't know him, and…"

"And what?"

*Ask me. I'll say yes.*

"I just don't want to stay with him," she finally says with a sigh.

We're both quiet as we pull into the parking lot at the shelter. I start to open my door but she clutches my wrist.

"I can do this by myself. I'll text you later."

Her eyes fill with tears but she seems determined.

"Come here," I mutter, hugging her to me over the center console. "I'll come get you tomorrow. We'll go to lunch or something. I'm always here. Just a phone call away if you need me." I kiss the top of her head. "This isn't goodbye, sweetheart. This is you spreading your wings a little. I'll still be here for you."

I cradle her cheeks as I pull away to look at her. My lips press to hers for a soft kiss. "I still want you with every fiber of my being. More time together. More of what we did last night and this morning. Okay?"

She swallows down her emotion and nods. "Okay."

"Don't drown," I say, as she pulls away and steps out of the car. I'm rewarded with a small smile that seems like it's more for show.

"I won't."

As she walks away, I can't help but think I'm sinking.

I'm the one who will drown without her.

Which means I need to figure out a way to get Cora and bring my girls home where they belong. Jenna's not some wishy-washy teen. She's responsible, mature beyond her years, and so deserving of constant people in her life who care about her. She really does belong with me, and I won't allow my self-doubt to infringe upon that.

With determination surging through me, I watch her enter the building, and then pull out of the parking lot on a mission. I'm going to find a way.

I walk into the pub and find August in a booth in the back. His head is bowed as he texts, a small smile on his face. August and I are acquaintances, having met on several cases. It wasn't until recently that we've gone out for a beer here and there as actual friends. I sure as hell need a friend right now to help me sort through this shit.

"Tauber," he says in greeting before shoving his phone in his pocket and meeting my stare.

"Miller," I grunt. "What has you smiling? I didn't know your mouth knew that maneuver."

He flashes me a million-dollar smile and his eyes darken with wickedness. "My mouth knows plenty of moves. Just ask my girl."

"Girl, huh?"

Embarrassment on August is new. His cheeks turn pink for a moment before he shrugs. "I'm with someone much younger. Got a problem?"

"How much younger?" I probe.

"She's eighteen," he says in a defensive tone.

I let out a relieved sigh. Maybe he'll understand what I'm going through. "I have a problem and I need help."

"So you said earlier."

A waitress comes by and August orders a couple of house drafts.

"Go on," he urges.

I rub at the back of my neck and let out a ragged sigh. "One of my kids…" Sourness roils in my stomach. This is probably going to sound sketchy as fuck when he learns I'm sleeping with her. "One of my kids, Jenna, wants to adopt one of my other kids, Cora."

His eyes narrow. "I remember them. Nick and Dane went with you to see them at Christmas. The boys too."

"Jenna just turned eighteen, and she thinks…" I trail off because it sounds impossible to my own ears, so I know it will to him.

"She thinks she'll magically be able to sign on the dotted lines and get the little girl, huh?"

"I told her it wasn't that simple. Too many factors involved." I know a little of the adoption process, but usually, I'm on the opposite side of it. In this case,

Cora's side. While it isn't my decision, my home stud-
ies and other assessments aid in the judge's decision.

"The law states the applicant must be twenty-one," he says, making me deflate. "But sometimes
that can be overruled in extraordinary cases."

"So, she can still hope?"

"She can. Age doesn't necessarily rule her out.
Mainly, she needs to have a permanent residence
established. The women's shelter won't work." He
frowns. "Does she have a job?"

The waitress delivers our beer and scampers off. I
sit up in my seat and take a sip before nodding. "Yeah.
Physical therapy clinic as a receptionist. She starts
Monday after school. It's part-time."

He takes a long pull from his beer and his brows
furl as he thinks. Finally, he relieves me of the suspense of what's going on his head. "Every situation is
different, but it all boils down to the agency's approval
and the judge at the finalization hearing. While the
rules state adoption isn't discriminatory on age, income level, and marital status, ultimately, the agency
will decide yay or nay. It'd be in your best interest to
help her line everything up, so we'd have the best case
in getting the adoption approved."

"We?" I say, smiling.

He snorts. "Don't act so surprised. I can be chari-
table sometimes."

"Thanks, man." I take another sip of beer and

then meet his stare. "So, give me the rundown. If I can give Jenna a plan she can follow, I think that will help."

"Six months. No agency will approve her without six months of stability, at the very least. They'll be sympathetic to their already-existing relationship and Jenna's having lived within the system all these years. Cora's caseworker," he says, pointing at me, "will perform a home study, perhaps periodically, to show proof of a stable home. It would be great to have some testimonials from well-trusted people in the community, if possible. Jenna's most recent foster parent, friends, co-workers, et cetera. They may even require a drug test if they're being hard on her. So tell her to keep her head on her shoulders, get a stable home, and don't get fired. Then, she could apply at that point. Applying now would be a waste of everyone's time. It'll get thrown out before even getting looked at."

I deflate because she won't like that answer. "I appreciate this. I'll do whatever it takes to help her."

He leans forward and his brows furl together. "Remember your place in her case. You're Cora's social worker. Your duty is to look out for Cora's best interest. I can see it in your lovesick eyes. You're either fucking the girl or getting your heart set on it. You're a grown ass man, so you can do whatever you want, but know that if it gets out and exposed, that could be a threat, not only to your job, but for any chance she has at getting Cora. I'm just being straight with you."

"So, moving in with me is out of the question."

He barks out a laugh. "Absolutely out of the question, man." He taps the side of his head. "Use your brain, not your dick. Help her secure an apartment or some shit. Don't move her in with you. It'll only complicate everything."

As much as I want to be her hero and save the day, I have to be smart about this. Begrudgingly, I pull out my phone and text the one person who can help.

**Me: Are you free tomorrow?**

His affirmative response is immediate.

I lie in bed in the dark, thinking about Jenna. Earlier, I'd called to check to see how she was acclimating to the women's shelter and wanted to discuss what August had told me. I managed to explain his plan of action and the six-month timeline before she told me she had to go. Her voice was shaky and I know she was on the verge of tears. I wish she were in my bed right now, so I could assure her everything would be okay. It has to be okay. I won't let it be any other way.

My phone rings, finally, and I pick up the call with a barked, "Hello."

"Hey," Jenna says, her voice lacking emotion.

"How are things?"

She lets out a soft sigh. "I'm just sitting in the closet. The closets here stink too."

I chuckle. "Maybe for your birthday, I should have bought you air freshener."

"Ha," she deadpans. "I think I prefer the new panties and bras instead."

My cock jolts at the memory of her trying them on for me in the dressing room earlier today. Her body is tight and lean, but her tits are jiggly and enticing. I'd enjoyed the hell out of watching them bounce in her new, prettier bras.

"I miss you," I tell her, my voice gruff as I attempt to push away thoughts of her nearly naked.

"I miss you too." A pause. "Enzo, I'm devastated." She silently cries on the other end, and I hate that I can't hold her.

"I know, baby. Shhh," I coo. "Everything is going to work out. You just have to trust me. It'll take time, which sucks, but Cora is worth it."

She stifles her sobs and chokes out her words. "S-She is, b-but it's b-breaking m-me not seeing her."

"When do you get out of work on Monday?"

"They close at seven, and Drew said everyone is usually out of there by seven thirty."

"I'll call Patty and see if we can come by around seven forty-five. You can see Cora before she goes to bed."

She sniffles. "Thank you. Yes, I'd love that."

"Now, about tomorrow."

"I want to see him. I'm ready."

"Are you ready to take this stranger up on his offer?"

"Between us," she mutters, "it terrifies me. But he seemed nice and he's a doctor. He can't be that bad. Plus, you'll come get me if it gets too bad, right?"

"Absolutely," I assure her. "I had Sheriff run a background check on him too. The guy is a good guy."

"Six months," she breathes. "I can do this."

"If anyone can, it's you, sweetheart."

"Enzo…"

"Mmm?"

"Thank you for everything. I know this is hard for you. I'm putting your job in jeopardy just by being with you."

"You're worth it, Jenna," I growl, a little too fiercely. "And I intend on proving to you that very thing. Trust me, and we'll get through this together. I want you and Cora to be happy."

She's quiet for a moment.

"I don't think I'd have lasted here long anyway," she mutters. "Some of the women here are really nice. But a few…" She trails off. "A few seem to not like me. One girl told me to stop staring at her. I wasn't even looking at her. And when I didn't answer her, she shoved me into a wall and told me to watch my fucking attitude."

I cringe at hearing yet another person hurt my sweet Jenna.

"I'm sorry," I choke out, guilt threatening to suffocate me.

"Don't be sorry," she whispers. "It was you in my head that kept me from kicking that girl in the boob. *Don't drown*. So, I lifted my chin and got the hell away from her. I may feel like I'm sinking, but I'm a pretty good swimmer when it comes to life."

I smile. "There's my girl."

"Can you come get me in the morning?"

"First thing. We'll have breakfast and then later, we'll go see Daniel. Hang in there, babe."

"I'll do my best."

We hang up after our goodbyes and I stare up at the dark ceiling. Halo hops on the bed, sensing my wakefulness, and purrs as he snuggles at my side.

"It's going to work," I tell my cat.

He meows in the bored way he's perfected. *Of course it will.*

# fourteen

*Jenna*

"Holy crap," I hiss when we pull into the driveway of my father's home.

Enzo squeezes my hand. "He's a doctor, remember?"

"A really rich one," I say with a snort. "Why does he have such a big house if it's just him?"

"Maybe he hoped one day he could fill it up," he says wistfully.

My heart does a little flutter, knowing Enzo's house is too big for him too. It has a couple of extra bedrooms, and I wonder if he hopes to fill his place up one day as well.

"I'm nervous about this," I admit as we climb out. "What if he turns out to be a major dick?"

Enzo stops me and cradles my face with his palms. His intense hazel eyes bore into me. He plants a sweet kiss to the corner of my mouth. "You tell me if he even looks at you weird. I'll get you out of there so fast your head will spin."

I turn my head slightly to meet his lips so he can kiss me deeper. His tongue swipes along mine, sending a thrill shooting down my spine. "And where will you take me?"

He tugs on my bottom lip with his teeth before flashing me a wolfish grin. "Where I absolutely shouldn't."

My heart stutters in my chest. "Where's that?"

"My home."

The thought is enticing. It'd be so much easier to let Enzo take care of me. But he warned me of what August had said. That if the judge figured out I was living with my old caseworker, it could really blow apart any chance I have of getting Cora. Everything would turn into a big mess, which is exactly what I'm trying to avoid. Of course life wouldn't be so simple. But Cora is worth trudging through the crap to get to. My chest aches as I think about my little angel. I miss her smile, and her adorable face, and her scent. Tears swim in my eyes.

"You'll be okay," Enzo assures me. "You're doing this for Cora." I love when he seems to reach inside my brain and find my exact thoughts.

"For Cora," I mimic as we start for the front door.

Before we reach the door, it swings open and Daniel greets us. I can't help but notice similarities between us. This is surreal. I go my entire life with no one and then suddenly, I have a dad who wants to be in my life. I'm not sure how to feel about it all.

"Jenna," he says, a nervous smile on his face. "I'm so happy you decided to come here rather than stay at the shelter. Whatever you need, just ask. I want to make up for all the time we lost together."

My heart melts at his words. The tears that had been brimming earlier spring back up. So often, I try to be tough and hard, but lately, I feel like my walls are crumbling around me. I'm exposed to these people, and I have to trust they don't hurt what they find.

I walk over to him and give him an awkward hug. At first, he's stiff, but then he hugs me tight, as though he's afraid I might disappear or change my mind. He's my blood. My family. And to have him hugging me back with such vigor makes something crack deep inside of me. Something frozen splits down the middle and bleeds warmth. I choke out a sob of relief. I'd come here for other reasons—for Cora—but right now, I feel like I'm doing it for me. I need this.

"Oh, honey," he says softly. "I'm so sorry for everything you've had to endure. But I swear, if you'll let me, I'll be the best dad a girl could have."

Sniffling, I nod against him, thankful he wants this relationship as much as I do. I don't get any creepy vibes from him. No, I feel hope radiating from him in waves. A hope that matches my own.

"Come on inside," he says, a smile in his voice. "I

have a lasagna in the oven and it's almost ready."

"You can cook?" I ask, astonished as I pull away.

He chuckles. "And clean, and even knit if you can believe it."

Enzo snorts and I let out a laugh.

"Knit?" My brow lifts at him, not able to continue without an explanation.

His smile is warm. "My mom taught me. Said men need to know how to do everything. To find them a good wife one day." He chuckles. "While she's still holding out on the wife part from me, she's over the moon that I'm able to give her a granddaughter."

His words sink in and I gape at him. "I have a grandma?"

"You do, and she's dying to meet you. I told her to let you have some time to settle in before she barges in and spoils you rotten." He smirks at that thought. "My mother is over the top."

"She sounds sassy. I like her already," I say with a grin.

"Sassy is an understatement."

Lunch was surprisingly wonderful. Daniel, or Dad, as he wants me to call him, is funny and nice. I really like him a lot. And I could see Enzo relaxing visibly after a while, once he realized my father is a good guy.

I'm actually excited to stay with him rather than the shelter.

"Let me show you to your rooms," Dad says, as we put away the last of the food.

We follow him through the nice home. The walls are light gray and the wood floors are a dark gray. His furniture is modern rustic, but it all looks comfortable and inviting. I like his decorating style, for sure. I'm anxious to see my room.

"This here is a small study," he says, pointing inside the room. "I thought you could do your homework in there if you want. I already hooked up a laptop. It's mine, but we can order one for you later."

I step inside the small space and marvel at how cute it is. There's a wooden desk with a trendy lamp on it, and built-in bookcases along one wall, filled with books. I walk over to them and notice they're medical books. It makes me curious to crack one open, but I'll have to investigate later on my own. The other side of the room has a small bar area. But instead of liquor, there are baskets with snacks. It has a tiny sink and a little built-in refrigerator beneath the cabinet.

"And this here is Cora's room," he says, ushering us out of the study. "If she ever gets to visit. We can buy her some toys and stuff to keep in here. I want her to feel welcome too."

My throat burns with emotion and I have to

blink away my tears. Enzo places a comforting hand on my shoulder.

"That's a nice gesture," Enzo says to Dad.

Dad walks us through Cora's room to a bathroom. It's white from floor to ceiling, with a giant clawfoot bathtub in the center. Then, he guides us through another door that leads into a bigger bedroom. "This is your room."

The bed is a large one—a king-size one, if I had to guess. It has giant open windows that overlook the greenbelt behind Dad's home. But what has me grinning happily are the French doors that lead to a small back patio.

"Wow," I utter in disbelief. "This is so nice. Thank you."

Dad nods at me, a sheepish smile on his face. "I just want this to feel like your home, because it is now."

"It's beautiful," I murmur. "Thank you for taking me in and wanting a relationship with me. It's a little too much to handle at the moment, but I'm happy. I want you to know that."

He nods. "I'm happy too, honey."

I walk over to the French doors and open them. It's almost like having my own little apartment.

"I'll let you unpack your stuff," Dad says. "I'll be in the kitchen, washing up the dishes. You can come back in there when you're done, and we can see about ordering you what you need. Clothes, shoes, whatever you need."

I give him a watery smile and then he's gone, closing the door behind him. As soon as we're alone, Enzo pulls me into his arms.

"How are you holding up?" he asks, his hot breath tickling the top of my head.

"Amazingly well," I admit. "I'm excited. Nervous, but excited. Is it too good to be true?"

He pulls away slightly and smiles at me. "After the life you've lived, it's hard not to be cynical. Trust me, I understand. But sometimes, people truly are just good. Like Daniel. He's a nice guy who just learned he has a daughter. I think he wants this relationship every bit as much as you, and he's trying to do right by you now." He kisses my forehead. "Just let the good happen, Jenna."

I sink into his embrace. I'm so used to trying to control every bit of my life that I can. And not much of it is good. So, to sit here and just allow good stuff to happen to me, without having to be in control, is a new experience. One I'm going to have to get used to, that's for sure.

"Hey," a voice says from behind me, jolting me from my inner panic.

I turn to find Sophia Rowe watching my meltdown with an arched brow. Today's my first day and Drew, the owner of this physical therapy clinic, gave me minimal instructions before setting me free on my own. I've been struggling ever since, but he's been too busy with patients for me to bug.

"Hi," I grumble. "Any chance you know why the screen is frozen?"

She limps over to me and bangs on the keys a few times to no avail. "Nope."

A giggle slips past my lips as she sits in a chair next to me. "Uh, thanks for nothing. Drew's going to be mad I broke his computer."

"I'll distract him from his anger," she vows, waggling her brows suggestively at me. "I have my ways."

Sophia is young, maybe close to my age, but I'm pretty sure she and Drew have a thing going on. Nobody has come out and told me for sure, being the newbie here and all, but I've watched his eyes track her, like he wants to pin her down and take a bite of her.

"Are you two dating?" I ask.

She snorts at my words. "Ehhh, something like that." One of the other physical therapists looks our way and then attempts to rush away, but Sophia stops her by hollering out her name. "Johnna! Come here for a sec."

Johnna winces and shoots us a wary stare.

"She hates me," Sophia mutters under her breath. "Everyone does."

"Except Drew," I point out. "He looks like he wants to eat you."

Sophia's lips curl into a wicked smile. "Oh, he totally wants to eat me. Sometimes I let him." She winks at me before barking at Johnna again. "Today, Johnna. The system is frozen."

Johnna lets out a sigh and purses her lips before making her way over to us. Sophia seems to enjoy the older woman's nervousness around her. It reminds me of Winter. Winter likes lording her badass attitude over everyone around her. Sophia and Winter would like each other.

"After you book the appointment, you have to hit the 'save draft' button and not the 'continue' button. For some reason, that's the only way it'll save the appointment and not freeze up," Johnna explains. "When it gets like this, you have to restart your computer and input it all over again."

She helps me get it restarted and after I input the information once more, it lets me move on after I hit the right button.

"Thanks," Sophia says. "Now you better go on or you're going to hear some sex talk. We were talking about eating puss—"

"No! I don't need to hear about it." Johnna pales. "You can, uh, keep that to yourself."

"Are you sure you don't want to hear about Drew's tongue—"

"Dear God, no," Johnna groans, backing away.

"Thank you for helping me," I tell Johnna, and try to smother my laugh.

As soon as the woman is gone, Sophia chuckles. "She's so uptight. I like making her cringe. Once, she walked in on us. Drew's fingers weren't being so innocent, if you know what I mean."

"She walked in on him fingering you?" I hiss. "Oh my God. That's so embarrassing. What did you guys do?"

Sophia shrugs. "Drew told her he'd be out in a minute, and then he proceeded to give me an orgasm that I would never forget." Her grin is evil. "Johnna pretends she saw nothing, despite how I like to nag her about it now."

"You totally thrive on terrorizing people, huh?"

"Totally," she says happily. "Oh, God. Would you look at him? Why does he have to be so stupid hot? I'm mad at him. But look. How the hell am I supposed to be mad when his butt looks like that in khakis?"

I follow her gaze as Drew is bent over a machine, showing a lady how to use it.

"He does have a nice butt," I tell her with a giggle.

"Damn right, he does." Then she points out the glass doors. "And so does that guy."

I find her checking out another nice ass in slacks.

Enzo's ass. He's on the phone just outside the door, and his butt does look pretty bite-able today.

I shove her with my shoulder. "That's my…boy-friend." I mean, I guess he is. We had sex and are completely into each other. Even without labeling our relationship prior to now, that's what he feels like to me.

"No way," she hisses. "He's old!"

"Like *your* boyfriend?"

"Yeah, you got a point there." She huffs in faux annoyance. "Why are the older ones so damn sexy? They're bossy too. Just so you know. I think they get into the whole daddy kink."

"How does he put up with you and that mouth of yours?" I tease. I like Sophia, even though everyone else seems to avoid her like the plague.

Leaning in, she whispers, "Because this mouth of mine is really good at sucking dick."

"Sophia!" I shriek.

Drew turns our way and smirks. He doesn't seem mad, though. Maybe he's a little happy she's making someone laugh and not pissing anyone off for the first time this afternoon.

"We were just talking about how old you were," she calls out to him.

The lady on the machine laughs.

Unfazed, all he does is mouth the word "later" to her before going back to his task of helping the woman.

"You're in trouble," I warn, grinning.

"When am I *not* in trouble?" she retorts back. "Now tell me about Mob Daddy out there. Is he with the Italian mafia? He's totally got a *Godfather* vibe going on."

"He's a social worker," I say.

"By day," she utters. "And by night?"

"Just Enzo."

"Italian lover."

I laugh. "He's definitely good at that. Although, we've only spent one night together."

He must feel our eyes on him because he turns to regard us through the windows. His smile is immediate upon seeing me.

"Daaaamn," she drawls out. "You scored big, J. He's totally big, right? I mean, the way his pants are hugging his dic—"

Her words get caught in her throat when someone covers her mouth with his hand. Drew. Once her mouth is sealed shut, he covers her eyes too. While she squirms, he addresses me.

"How'd your first day go?" he asks, not worried that she's slapping at his arms and throwing a fit.

I stifle a laugh. "It was fun. Learned lots. Thank you for letting me work here. Means a lot." I point at Sophia. "The people here are great too."

His smirk fades as he flashes me a genuine smile, one filled with gratitude. "This brat likes to cause trouble and doesn't make friends too easily. Having you here will keep her out of my hair." He releases her and then ruffles her hair, messing it up. "Go clean the toilets or something," he tells her. "Make yourself useful around here."

She sticks her tongue out at him. "Meet me in the bathroom, and I'll show you how useful I can be."

His features darken. "Time for you to go home, Soph."

"Gladly," she purrs and stands. She limps over to him and pats his chest. "See you soon." Then, to me, she says, "I'll text you later. I'm gonna need deets on the mafia man."

Drew grumbles at her words. "Go away."

With a little wave, she hobbles away from us.

"Is she okay?" I ask, indicating her limping.

"She's a big crybaby," he groans. "She's definitely not okay." He says it affectionately, though. "Go on and get out of here. I see your *mafia man* is waiting."

My cheeks heat at his words and I mumble out my goodbye. When I make it outside, Enzo is frowning.

"Everything okay in there?" he asks. His jaw clenches and his stare remains inside.

"Yeah," I tell him, patting his chest. "My boss is in love with a very sassy girl. They're funny to watch."

He relaxes and turns his attention my way. His fingers run through my hair and he drops a kiss to my lips. "You ready to see Cora?"

"Absolutely."

# fifteen

*Enzo*

*Two weeks later…*

"La la la," Jenna calls out over her shoulder. "I can't hear you."

Her friend Sophia hobbles after her like an old woman, an evil grin splitting her face. "Cum. Everywhere. That's all I'm saying."

I widen my eyes at Jenna. "Umm…what?"

"Don't ask," she says with a snort.

"Call you later to give you all the juicy bits, J," Sophia hollers out.

Jenna laughs and flips her off before hopping into my car. I'm just opening my door to get in when Sophia turns her wickedness my way. "Don't worry, I'll hear all about your juicy bits too." With those words, she cackles and goes back inside the therapy clinic.

I climb in next to Jenna and shoot her a questioning look that only makes her giggle.

"Ugh, ignore her. You know how she is. Can we pick up slushees for the girls?" She buckles her seatbelt and starts flipping through her phone.

I can't help but smile. These past two weeks have done a number on her. She's no longer the sad girl she once was. Daniel has given her a home and his adoring attention. She has a job she loves and has made some great friends. And she has me. When we can, we steal away to my house to make love and hang out. The only thing missing to complete her life is Cora.

Thankfully, Patty lets us come by whenever we want. So, each day after Jenna gets out of work, we head over to see Cora and the other girls. The first day when we left, Cora bawled her eyes out. But now that she knows we're coming, it's easier for her to say goodbye to Jenna each day.

I run through a drive through to get everyone slushees. When we arrive at Patty's, the girls are thrilled to have been brought a treat.

Jenna sits on the sofa and Cora crawls into her lap. Like every other day we've come, they chatter about whatever it is those two talk about while Patty and I converse over Cora's well-being.

"She loves her," Patty says, before sipping her slushee. "Jenna may only be eighteen, but she loves Cora more than any parent ever could."

I glance over at Jenna. Cora is holding up her drink for Jenna to taste. Jenna pretends it's too sour, making Cora giggle, but she keeps making her taste it. They're adorable.

"She does. I hope one day they can be together again," I say softly.

Patty nods. "Me too, Mr. Tauber. Sometimes the law doesn't understand love. It has rules for love." She pats my knee and gives me a knowing smile. "But love is lawless. Love is unaware of social norms. Love doesn't give a damn."

I smirk. "Nope," I agree. "Love just does whatever it wants."

We spend a couple of hours with Cora and the girls until it's past bedtime. Cora is teary-eyed when we leave, but she doesn't throw a fit. Jenna is handling their parting much better than in the beginning. Still, as I drive her to her house, she's somber.

"You okay?"

She nods. "As okay as I can be."

I was going to take her to dinner and a movie, like we sometimes do after leaving Cora, but tonight feels like she might need a shoulder to cry on. We drive through and grab some burgers before heading to her house. In the car, we sit and eat them in silence.

"Can you come in?" she asks. Her brows are furled together. "Will you stay the night with me?"

I glance toward the house. Daniel is a nice guy, but I don't know how he'd feel about me spending the night. I don't want to do anything to jeopardize her relationship with her dad.

She laughs. "Relax. He's not going to come after you with a shotgun. I got a text earlier. He's been called in and won't be home until late tomorrow." Her smile is sexy. "It's just us."

"Then I'll stay," I tell her, flashing her a grin. "Now that I know I'm not going to get my nuts shot off."

We climb out of the car and I follow her around to the back of the house. She likes going in the back patio door to her room. I think it makes her feel like it's more her place that way. As soon as we enter, she pushes in the alarm code and throws her bag down on the floor. She closes the door and locks us in, as my gaze skims over her room. It's transformed since we first arrived. She's decorated it in teals and grays that are more her style than the masculine look it had before. Pictures of her and Cora litter the space and her clothes are strewn on the floor. The thing that has me curious is the stack of books on her nightstand.

"Been reading your dad's books?" I ask, as I pick up one of the medical books.

Her cheeks turn pink. "Was just seeing if it interested me enough to go to school for."

Pride thumps inside my chest. "Medical school? Like Daniel?"

"Maybe it runs in the family." She shrugs. "Drew's been letting me follow him around as he sees patients when we're slow up front. He says I pay attention better than Soph."

I set the book down. "I think you'd be great at it. You're great with all Cora's ailments."

"We'll see," she says in a noncommittal tone. "I'll do whatever is best for Cora. Even if it means working at the clinic full-time rather than going to college. You know she's my main priority."

Her words, while sweet and genuine, nag at me. I grab her hips and pull her close. "You can have your dreams *and* a family. You realize that, right?"

"One of those too-good-to-be-true scenarios," she murmurs.

"I'm just saying that—"

She presses her thumb to my lips. "How about we not talk about my future and talk about the present?" Her brow lifts as her other hand slides to grip me through my slacks. "How presently, I want to show you how thankful I am that you're such a good, doting boyfriend."

My dick jerks to life in her grip, throbbing in anticipation.

"Jenna," I rumble, my voice husky with need.

"Shhh," she whispers, as she starts unbuttoning my shirt. "All I want to hear are sounds of pleasure coming from you."

I groan at her sassy words. "What has gotten into you?"

"Not you…yet."

She pushes my shirt down my arms and it falls to the floor. Next, she rids me of my undershirt. My dick is straining against my slacks. Her fingers deftly unbuckle my belt and within seconds, she pushes my pants and underwear down. As if eager to see her, my cock bounces out in front of her, already leaking pre-cum at the tip.

Her tongue darts out and she licks her bottom lip. "Someone is awfully quiet now," she purrs.

She pulls off her sweater and then unhooks her bra. Her full tits are gifted to me for my visual tasting as she kneels before me. Her green eyes dart up to look at me. Confidence drips from her, and I thank God she's made friends with Sophia and Winter. Those two girls are instrumental in pulling her out of her shell. Self-assurance is a sexy quality on Jenna.

Her hand wraps around my cock, and she teases me by gently stroking me. I'm about to tell her to stop fucking with me when her tongue slides across my tip. My fingers slide into her hair, gripping her tight, and I let out a low growl.

"Fucking hell, Jenna."

She smiles, her tongue circling my tip, before she slides down over my length. A couple of times, she's given me head, but it's not anything I've actively asked for. But now that she's feeling sure in her abilities, and doing a damn good job, I might be inclined to suggest this in the near future.

My eyes snap closed when she gags slightly. I'm too large for her to take me fully in her mouth, but the beautiful girl tries. Fuck, how she tries. Slobber runs down my shaft to my balls, and my nerves are on fire with lust. As she sucks and teases my cock, her hand slides down my length, smearing her saliva. She rubs it over my balls, sending pleasure nearly exploding from me. My knees keep buckling as I nearly lose control. I manage to sputter out my words in warning.

"I'm going to come, sweetheart."

She slides off of me and murmurs, "Let me taste you."

Her words are my undoing, but it's her wicked green eyes that turn me the fuck on. She opens her swollen, pouty lips and sticks out her tongue, as though she's waiting on a treat. Then, she jacks me off with her wet hand. When I groan, a signal of my impending orgasm, she points my tip right at her open mouth. I hiss in pleasure and my cum shoots from me. It coats her tongue, thick and white. Her mouth latches onto the tip once more, and she swallows every drop until she's drained me dry.

With my grip tight in her hair, I pull her to her feet and kiss her sexy mouth that still tastes like me. Before she can get too into the kiss, I twist her away from me. My hands make quick work at undoing her pants and shoving them down her thighs. As soon as her panties are pushed down too, I bend her over the bed, baring her perfect round ass at me.

"Little girl playing big games with big boys, hmmm?" I ask, my voice husky.

She squirms and wiggles her ass at me. "I'm a big girl. You're the one who needs to keep up."

My cock lurches at her words. I smack her ass, loving when it immediately blooms pink. "You're the one bent over the bed and at my mercy, sweetheart." I run my finger between her thighs and am pleased to find her cunt soaked. Pushing inside her to my knuckle, I can't help but realize how lucky I am to have this gorgeous woman to call mine.

"Are you going to fuck me or just tease me?" she taunts.

I slowly thrust my finger in and out of her. "Teasing is more fun."

As I slide one finger inside her, I let one of the other ones rub along her clit each time I move my hand. Her body trembles and shakes. Over and over again, I take her near the edge of ecstasy until she's whimpering and begging for release.

"Beg for my cock," I tell her, slapping her ass with my free hand.

She clenches around my finger and cries out, "Please! I need it!"

I pull my fingers from her, chuckling at her grumble, and manage to find one condom in my wallet. We've tried to play it safe, but sometimes it just doesn't happen like it should. I tear at the foil with my teeth and sheath my still-wet cock with the rubber. Then, I line my tip up with her opening, before slamming all the way in. She screams, her fists yanking at the bedspread, and her cunt grips me to the point of dizzying me with pleasure.

"You like it when I fuck you hard," I growl. "Don't you?" To drive home my words, I spread her cheeks apart so I can look at her ass, and thrust into her deep. Her ass presses against me, eager for me to take her as far as I can go. I wet my thumb with my tongue and then I press it against her puckered hole. She cries out in shock and then whimpers when I probe her there.

"Ahh!"

"Good girl," I growl. "I'm going to work you up to take my cock here one day."

She shudders and her pussy grows slicker with arousal. I fuck her ass with my thumb as I fuck her pussy with my cock, and slap her ass cheek with my other hand. Each time I whap her flesh, her ass and pussy clench around me. It drives me wild, making me grind into her harder, faster, fiercer.

"Touch your clit, Jenna. Make yourself come, just like I taught you," I growl, my hand gripping her ass cheek hard.

She releases the bedspread to finger herself. Each time she gets close, her pussy tightens around me. When she starts to come, I slide my thumb out of her and grip her breasts, yanking her back to my chest. I fuck her hard, holding her up just by my dick inside her and my hands on her tits. Her strangled cry as her orgasm detonates fuels my own. I groan, nipping my teeth at her shoulder as I drain out my release.

"Damn, woman," I grunt, now pressing sweet kisses to her shoulder. "Damn."

She laughs. "You exhaust me."

Sliding her off my cock, I set her to her feet. When I reach down to pull off the condom, it's gone.

"Fuck," I grumble. "The condom's gone."

"Gone?" she asks, frowning at me.

"Lie down and let me look for it."

She whirls around, her green eyes wide. "It's *inside* me?"

I kiss her parted mouth. "Just lie back and spread your legs. I'll get it. Trust me."

Her brows furl together but she obeys. She's hot as fuck, lying on her bed with her legs spread open. Jenna makes me feel young again. Like I could fuck her ten times in a day and never grow tired. I skim my eyes down her taut stomach to her pussy that's red from my abuse. The condom has vanished. I ease two fingers into her on a hunt for the rubber. She squirms a little, but lets me fish around for it. I manage to locate it and pinch it between my fingers before pulling it out. Her pussy drips with cum as I pull the condom back out.

"It's dry inside," I point out, wiggling it at her. I toss it on the bed next to her and then run my knuckle up her slit. "So that means all this went right inside with no barrier."

"It's not the first time you've come inside me," she says softly.

I grab her hands and pull her to stand up with me. "I'm not trying to get you pregnant, but it's a real possibility, with as many times as we've had sex. And you're still not on the pill."

"Are you mad at me?" Her nose turns pink at her vulnerable question.

With a grin I can't fight, I kiss her gorgeous mouth. "No, but you have to understand something. I've been to college. I have my career. I'm ready to settle down. You, on the other hand, have so much out in front of you." I rest my forehead against hers. "I'm not going anywhere, but it's you I worry about. I don't want to take away your decisions by forcing a life-changing moment on you."

Her palms cup my scruffy cheeks. "I understand the consequences and repercussions. I'm still here. You have to remember that I'm not like most girls my age. We have very similar wants and desires."

A wicked grin curls my lips up. "Good, because I only had the one useless condom and if I'm staying the night, I plan on making love to you a helluva lot more times than once."

# sixteen

*Jenna*

*Two and a half months later…*

"He bought you a car?" Winter demands on the other line. "Seriously?"

"Is it weird?" I ask, gnawing on my bottom lip. "He said it was a graduation gift."

She laughs. "I mean, he *is* your dad and all, but you hardly know him. Did he seem weirded out to be giving it to you?"

"No," I tell her. "He seemed so happy."

"Well, that's sweet then," she says, and then she grumbles at someone. Then a squeal. "Shit! I have to go! Speaking of old daddies—" Her laugh is the last thing I hear before we get disconnected.

We learned that the attorney who's been helping me through Enzo is her boyfriend. Talk about a small world. She doesn't talk a ton about their relationship, though. All I know is she lives with him and he used to be her dad's best friend. There's all sorts of drama wrapped up in her life, so I try to give her a safe space from it all. We end up talking about my drama instead.

Enzo is the good kind of drama. He's doting in public and dominating in the bedroom. We squabble over silly things, but never anything that lasts.

The drama that's stressful for me revolves around Cora. Waiting for this six-month time period is ridiculous. She always asks me to come home or to go "bye-bye" with me. Thankfully, between my dad scheduling her ENT surgery and Patty following through with it, Cora now has the tubes she desperately needed. I asked Patty after Cora recovered if we could bring her over to Dad's to show her the room, but she didn't think it was a good idea. I cried myself to sleep that night.

I'm a high school graduate, and I've been accepted to a local college with a full scholarship. I have a car, and now, with school over, a full-time job. Everything is nearly perfect. Which is why the other day, I went down to the agency and filed the paperwork to get my girl.

Three months in one spot seems like more than enough time. I just want her home with me. My eyes water just thinking about Cora. I see her nearly every day, but it's not enough. I miss her so much.

Dad knocks on my open door and steps through the threshold. Today, he's in full-on doctor mode. All he's missing is his white lab coat. But he's wearing the intense, super focused look on his face that he reserves for work.

"Morning," he says. "Or should I say afternoon?"

I laugh and toss a pillow at him. "It's Sunday. Surely a girl can sleep in."

"Well, you missed breakfast, sleepyhead. I left it on the stove for you. I'm on my way out."

The mention of food has my stomach roiling. I curl up my lip and close my eyes.

"Everything okay?" Dad rumbles, suddenly on the bed beside me, checking my temperature like I'm eight instead of eighteen. He's a very devoted parent, I'm learning.

"Yeah, just feel crummy this morning."

He gives me a sympathetic smile. "Nervous?"

"It's been, like, three days since I filed the application. I haven't heard a word back."

"These things take time. I'm sure everything's fine."

"Thanks, Dad."

He looks at his watch. "Is Enzo coming over today?"

"Later. He had to go to his mom's to help them trim some trees. I'll tell him you said hi. When will you be home?"

"Not until tomorrow afternoon. If you need me though, text me. I'm just around the corner."

I smile at him. "I won't bug you at work."

"But you know you can, right? No matter what?"

My heart swells. It's nice having family. This feeling will never get old. "I know."

He pats my head. "Good. Gotta go, kiddo. See you tomorrow."

As he makes his way toward the door, I'm overcome with emotion. I burst from the bed and hug him from behind. "I love you."

His voice is choked when he responds. "Love you too, Jenna."

I wake to the ringing of my phone. My first thought is that it's Enzo, but then I remember he was out late helping his mom and just went home to crash, knowing he had to be up early for work. The number isn't one I recognize. It's a little after eight, and I groan when I realize I've slept through my alarm. I'm supposed to be at work already. Crap.

"Hello?" I answer absently as I climb out of bed.

"Miss Pruitt?"

"This is her."

"Hi, this is Candace from the Families First Adoption agency."

My heart rate quickens. "Hello," I say in my perkiest voice, despite the fact I want to throw up from nerves.

"I just wanted to let you know we received your application, and…" She trails off. "I'm sorry but at this time, it's been denied."

Time freezes as I process her words. "W-What?"

"It was denied based on length of employment and length of residency."

"But I've been here three months," I argue, my words shrill.

"I'm sorry."

"No," I snap. "I need more answers."

"Listen, dear, I'll be real honest with you. Even though age isn't supposed to be a factor, because the law is negotiable where that is concerned depending on certain factors, it's a silent denial here. Anyone under the age of twenty-one is. If you were to wait until then, maybe—"

"I'm not waiting until my daughter turns five to get her back!" I screech, tears spilling down my cheeks.

"With all due respect, she's not your daughter, Miss Pruitt."

I choke on a sob. "C-Can you run it again? I c-can get p-people to vouch f-for me. My b-boss. My dad. Please."

She lets out a heavy sigh. "I think your best bet would be to wait at least another nine months before applying again. Having a year under your belt will look good on the application."

I don't remember hanging up with her. Just crying. Crying and crying. And then getting sick. After throwing up my guts, I return to my phone to discover I have missed calls from the physical therapy clinic, some texts from Sophia, and a few from Enzo.

**Sophia: You're late, hooch.**

**Sophia: Seriously, where are you?**

**Sophia: Is everything okay?**

**Enzo: Good morning, sweetheart.**

**Enzo: Mom sent me home with some pie. I'll bring it by later.**

**Enzo: Call me…it's not like you not to answer.**

I reply to Sophia and tell her I'm sick. I'm about to reply to Enzo, but he calls me this time.

"Hey," he greets.

All I can do is sob in response.

"Jenna," he growls. "What's wrong?"

My chest feels like there's a hole in it. "I'm just having a bad day is all." I can't tell him. Not until I calm down. He'll be angry for me applying when he specifically told me to wait.

"As soon as I make a home visit, I'll come to you. Are you at work?" he demands.

"I'm at home," I choke out. "I'm fine. Just call me later."

He's silent for a beat and then he blurts out his words. "I love you. Everything's going to be okay."

I cry harder at his words. Words he's never spoken to me before now. It only makes me feel more emotional. "I love you too."

I hang up the phone to rush to the bathroom again. Sitting on the cold tile floor, I feel sorry for myself as I dry heave. I manage a text to my dad.

**Me: Dad, I'm sick. And my heart is broken. They denied my application.**

He doesn't reply and I throw up again.

My hand shakes as I stare at the pregnancy test. I bought one the other day when I'd felt sick. I missed my period but I've been stressed about everything, so I chalked it up to that. And quite frankly, I was scared to take it. But now that I can't keep anything down, I decided to take the test.

There's no denying it.

Pregnant.

Instead of feeling elated, I feel even more upset. Like maybe this is the nail in the coffin of ever getting Cora. It's not fair. She's mine in every sense of the word. No one else wants her but me. So why won't they let me have her?

I need to see her.

If I see her, then I can get the strength to keep going. I just need to kiss her sweet face. I just need her to encourage me and remind me I can do this.

I'm brushing my teeth and running out the door before I know it. Maybe Patty will let me take her for a drive to the park or to lunch. I have the car seat ready for the day she's mine. Patty is nice and will understand I need to spend time with her.

I drive to Patty's and can barely contain my excitement when I knock on the front door. Delia eventually answers the door.

"Hey," she greets. "Cora's upstairs."

She makes her way back into the kitchen where I can hear Patty and Faye chattering about food. I bound up the steps, seeking out Cora. As soon as she sees me, she starts crying, which makes me cry. I rush over to her and pull her into my arms.

"My baby," I sob, kissing her sweet face. "I missed you."

We both cry and she hugs my neck so tight I can hardly breathe.

How dare the stupid agency keep me from the other half of my heart? My little banshee baby needs me. Her heart is broken, both of ours are. Being separated is killing us. They're so worried about their dumb laws, but what about the well-being of the child? What about her psychological health? This can't be healthy, leaving her abandoned with strangers.

"Go bye-bye with Mommy," Cora whines, nuzzling her head against my neck.

My mind races with that thought. And before I can think rationally, I'm snagging her koala bear from the bed and tucking it into her arms. I kiss her head and then silently walk her down the hall. Down the stairs. Out the front door.

Each step, the heavy weight on my shoulder lifts. Each step, I feel free.

We reach my car and I open the door, looking behind me. Nobody cares about her. Nobody loves her like I do. I sit her in the seat and buckle her in before handing her the bear. Then, I climb into the front seat. I wait. I wait for them to tell me no. I wait for them to realize she's more than just some kid. She's *my* kid. She deserves love and belonging. We deserve to be together.

My heart is racing in my chest as anxiety threatens to make me sick again. I ignore it all as I focus on driving back home. The drive is a blur. The walk to Dad's house is a blur. Pushing through the back door is a blur. The fog doesn't seem to lift until I set Cora down in her room. I've been buying her toys with my paychecks. Toys, clothes, stuffed animals. I've been filling her room for three months, waiting on this moment.

"This is your room, baby," I tell her tearfully. I point through the bathroom. "That's Mommy's room. We'll be close now."

She babbles and grins toothily at me as she finds

the pink piano in the corner. The banging gives me a headache, but it's worth it. I have her here with me. She plays for a little bit, but then whines because she needs a nap. We crawl into her bed and I tuck her beside me where I can inhale her head and whisper silly stories to her. Her breathing evens out and I find myself exhausted over the day's events.

This is bad.

I've done something very bad.

But with her here with me, it doesn't feel so bad.

I fall asleep and have nightmares of them taking her away. In my dreams, I claw and fight them to the death.

She's mine.

# seventeen

*Enzo*

y phone keeps buzzing in my pocket, but I can't answer it until I leave the house I'm doing a home study for. As soon as I sit down in my car, I answer, worried that Jenna is doing worse than she was this morning. Everything about her was strange earlier.

"Hello?"

"Oh, thank God, Mr. Tauber!"

"Patty? Is everything okay with Cora?"

She breathes heavily in the phone. "She's gone."

"Gone?" I demand, my voice rising. "Did you call the police? Did she walk off? She could be hurt!" Jenna will freak the fuck out. *I'm* freaking the fuck out.

"No," Patty says sadly. "I didn't call the cops. Yet. It's…"

"It's what?" I ask harshly.

"Delia said Jenna stopped by and then suddenly,

Cora's gone. I think she took her."

My heart ceases to beat in my chest. She wouldn't. Jenna wouldn't fuck up everything because she missed Cora. Something's wrong and I need to get to the bottom of it.

"Hang tight. I'm going to make some calls. I'll call you right back," I bark at her.

I haul ass toward Daniel's house and dial Jenna. She doesn't answer. Fuck. Before I call Sheriff McMahon, I need to make sure Jenna hasn't taken her. If she did, I need to do damage control. When I pull into the driveway at their house, I see her car is parked out front. I rush from the car and run to her back door. Using my key she had made for me, I let myself in. Her bed is empty, but I don't stop there. I storm through the adjoining bathroom to Cora's room. The sight stops me in my tracks.

Both girls.

Asleep.

Cora is curled up in Jenna's sleepy but protective embrace.

Fuckfuckfuckfuck.

I run my fingers through my hair and crack my neck before I make my way back to her room. I dial Patty back. She answers on the first ring.

"She's with Jenna," I hiss. "Let me fix this. Please."

"I was scared out of my mind," Patty croaks. "I thought somethin' had happened to that baby."

"I know," I breathe. "Let me find out what's going on. I'll bring Cora home soon. I promise."

She lets out a heavy sigh. "I'm sorry, Mr. Tauber. I wish things were easier for them."

"Me too."

We disconnect and I walk back in Cora's room. I pat Jenna's foot until she stirs and wakes. When her eyes meet mine, they're filled with relief. Then, as her situation dawns on her, she sits up in a panic.

"What are you doing here?" she demands, her shrill voice waking Cora.

"Sweetheart," I say gently. "You know why I'm here." I pinch the bridge of my nose. "Why? Why would you do this? You've screwed everything up."

She chokes on a sob, her bottom lip wobbling wildly. "I applied last week." Fat tears roll down her cheeks. "They denied me."

I sit down beside her and pull her against my chest. "Oh, Jenna. Why? Why didn't you just wait? Why did you go around me to do this? I am one of the few people who can help you."

She shrugs, a loud sob escaping her. Cora whines and I pull her between us to kiss her.

"It's okay, angel," I tell Cora. "Have you been having fun with Jenna?"

Cora nods and points to the bathroom. "Mommy room." Then she frowns at me. "My room."

"Soon, baby," I murmur. "But Patty is worried

about you. You have to go back there until Mommy gets everything ready."

"Nooo," Cora yells. "Stay with Mommy!"

Fuck.

Jenna, defeated, cries hard. I wish I could magically make all this better. But it's a clusterfuck of emotions and laws. No matter what I do, it'll be wrong for its own reasons.

"I have to take her back, Jenna," I say firmly. "Right now. Patty is a mess."

Jenna pulls back, shaking her head. "No. Please let her stay the night."

I frown at her. "I told her I'd be bringing her back. You know my job requires me to look after Cora. You've already jeopardized more than your chance at adoption. You're jeopardizing my career."

As though my words sting her, she jerks away from me and stands up. Cora scrambles over to her and latches onto Jenna. I rise and hold my hands out to them.

"You can see her again soon," I tell Jenna. "Please don't make me a villain over this. I'm trying to help you before it gets out of hand. Patty was about to call the police."

"Please don't take her," she begs. "Please, Enzo. I can't handle this. Not from you."

"It's either me or Sheriff McMahon." My heart aches at the sadness in her eyes, but I'm doing this for her. This isn't some fantasy world. If we don't take Cora back, Patty will call the police and they'll forcibly remove Cora, arrest Jenna, and I'll get fired. I know Jenna loves Cora with all her being, but I know she doesn't want to ruin everyone's lives over one mistake.

The door bursts open behind me and Daniel charges in.

"Jenna!" he bellows. "I've been worried sick about…" He trails off and lets out a sigh. "This must be Cora."

I grip his shoulder. He's still wearing his lab coat. "We have to get Cora back before the police get called." I flash him a heavy look, one that says, "Your daughter just kidnapped this kid and a shit storm is brewing." Luckily, understanding dawns in his eyes.

"Look what I have," Daniel tells Cora, reaching into his pocket. "A lollipop." He hands Cora the pink sucker and she smiles shyly at him.

"Doctor," she says to Jenna, pointing at him.

"Yes, doctor," Jenna whispers.

"Jenna," I mutter. "It's time."

Daniel frowns, but walks over to his daughter. He rubs her shoulders. "Say goodbye, honey."

Jenna sobs and shakes her head. She pulls Cora to her, crying. They kiss and hug. We give them a few minutes until I realize we'll be here all day if I don't make a move. And time is of the essence. I reach for Cora and have to pry her from Jenna's grip as Daniel holds her to him. Both girls scream. So many tears. My heart fucking shatters to have to do this to them.

I carry the screeching baby out of the house.

To the car.

Buckle her in despite her screaming and squirming.

And I take her back to Patty, leaving my heart on the floor by Jenna's feet.

I sit in my car outside of Daniel's house after having brought Cora back to Patty. Cora settled once she was back at the foster home. All the girls were crying over how upset she was and were trying to comfort her. Faye eventually won her heart with a cupcake. I left before I did something stupid, like take her back home with me. Now, I'm trying to get the courage to go see Jenna.

She hates me.

I felt it pouring from her as I pried that little girl from her arms.

But we averted a crisis. Patty said her lips were sealed but that it absolutely cannot happen again. I promised her it wouldn't. I sure as hell hope it doesn't.

**Daniel: How do we fix this?**

I stare at his text and shrug. I don't know. I don't fucking know. Scrubbing a hand down my face, I decide to go in and talk to him first. I find him inside, standing at the kitchen island, drinking a beer. As soon as he sees me, he walks over to the fridge and retrieves me one. He pops the cap off and hands it to me.

"How do we fix this?" he mutters, echoing his last text.

"I don't know."

"While you were gone, I talked to her. They denied her application. There has to be a better way, Enzo. How do we get that little girl back into my little girl's life? I'm afraid not being able to be permanently reunited with Cora is going to send my daughter down a dark path." He frowns and stares into his bottle. "Her mother was out of control. One of the things I admired about her, but also one of the things I detested about her. Drugs, alcohol, money. She was impulsive about everything. Until tonight, I was just sure Jenna had more of me in her. But seeing her meltdown over Cora and the look in her eyes that meant she felt justified in breaking such a big law made me realize she has more of her mother in her than I ever realized."

I take a long pull on my beer. "I guess we could take it to court. I would have suggested that before she resorted to kidnapping had she just talked to me about it," I grumble bitterly. "Now, everything is too fragile. I like Patty, but I don't know if we can trust her not to spill."

Daniel paces the floor in front of the refrigerator. "How hard is it to become a foster parent?"

"She's too young. They're not going to let her—"

"Not her. Me."

Hope flares inside my chest but I squash it down. "It's a serious commitment…"

He points toward the other end of the house. "That's my little girl in there. Her heart is breaking in two right now. If there's a chance I can mend it, you better believe I will."

"There are steps. It's not an overnight process. Forms and background checks," I warn him. "Questionnaires to make sure you're doing this for the right reason."

He straightens his back and nods at me. "Let's get started. I'll do what it takes. If I can foster Cora, then she can live here. With Jenna."

"I just hate to get her hopes up, man."

"Jenna is a tough girl. If we can fight for this, let's fight. If it means going dirty and finding a work-around the system, we'll find one. For my daughter. You love her, right?"

We haven't exactly hidden our relationship from him, and Daniel hasn't tried to keep her from me, but it still surprises me that he knows how much she means to me from simple outsider observation.

I give him a fierce nod. "So fucking much."

He smiles, pleased. "Good. Make this happen, Enzo. Do whatever it takes."

I'm already working out the puzzle in my head. Going over the time frame and papers that need to be filed. The works.

"Her best friend Winter's boyfriend is an attorney. Her other best friend's father is a judge," he tells me, a wide grin on his face. "Her boyfriend's a social worker and her dad's a pillar of the community. We're bringing Cora home to us, one way or another."

I drain the rest of my beer and set it down before extending my hand. We shake as though it's some multimillion dollar deal rather than the fate of two very special girls.

We'll bring her home.

I'm just sure of it.

I tiptoe into Jenna's bedroom after I helped Daniel fill out the paperwork. We submitted it to the proper channels, and I even called August to bring him up to date. While I'd cringed, waiting for him to yell about the whole kidnapping debacle, he didn't. Simply made a plan of action. The plan is to expedite the filings in order to make Daniel a foster parent. Then, we'll keep filing Jenna's adoption request until they can't deny her any longer. Even if we have to wait until she turns twenty-one. At least they'll be together, which is the most important part.

I undress down to my boxers and climb into bed. She may be furious at me for taking Cora home, but Jenna still loves me despite that. And right now, she needs my loving arms wrapped around her. Jenna is fierce and strong, but sometimes even she needs to break apart and let someone hold her back together.

"Hey, baby," I murmur as I wrap an arm around her.

She stiffens, but doesn't pull away. Soon, the bed shakes as she silently cries. I kiss her hair and whisper assurances.

*Don't drown. Don't drown. Don't fucking drown.*
*Let me save you.*

Eventually, her sobs die down and she turns to face me, burying her face against my chest.

"I'm sorry," she croaks.

I kiss the top of her head. "I'm sorry too. I didn't want to have to take her. You know that, Jenna."

She nods. "I know. I'm just an emotional mess. It's been a day from hell."

"Talk to me," I encourage. "I'm here."

Her body pulls away from mine, and then we're bathed in light from the bedside lamp. Brown hair that's usually smoothed straight is a tangled mess on her head. Glassy, bloodshot eyes peer back at me and her bottom lip wobbles. My sweet girl is breaking apart.

"Enzo," she says softly, taking my hand in hers. "I love you."

Seeing the words tumble from her lips is better than hearing them earlier on the phone. "I love you too, sweetheart. I've loved you for a long time."

Her lips tease at a smile, but then it fades. "I'm pregnant."

I stare at her for a moment, letting her words sink in. The sickness. The many times we fucked with no condom. The irrational, emotional behavior. It's all starting to come together.

"How do you feel about it?" I ask her softly, not wanting to sway my decision on her.

"Happy. Confused. Excited. Scared." She blinks and more tears roll down. "Mostly worried."

I sit up and draw her to me so I can kiss her trembling bottom lip. "I'll take care of you. Of both of you. You know this. I hope you're not worried about that. That should never have crossed your mind."

Relief glimmers in her eyes. "You're going to keep me? Even after I committed a major felony today, treated you like shit, and threatened your job?"

I guide her onto her back and lay stretched out beside her. My fingertip strokes down to her stomach and I circle her belly button over her shirt before settling my palm there. "I was always going to keep you," I tell her, pinning her with a fierce stare. "As soon as I brought you home with me, I knew I was going to keep you. I was worried you'd wake up one day though, and realize you haven't explored enough of the world. I wanted to let you make your own decisions, after having gone so long with other people making them for you."

She rests her hand on mine. "I don't need to see the world. My world's right here." Her lips tug into a frown. "Well, almost all of it."

I lean over and kiss her cheek. "We're going to get her. Until we can legally make her ours, we have options. It might be unusual and not like you'd originally planned, but we're going to figure it out."

"We?"

"As soon as you'll let me, I'm going to drag your pretty ass down to the courthouse and make you legally mine. Then we'll be an official 'we.'"

Her smile is breathtaking. "I'd let you take me right now."

"Is that a yes? I haven't even showed you the ring yet," I tease.

"I don't need a ring," she says, her loving eyes brimming with tears. "Just you."

Leaning forward, I nip at her bottom lip. "Well, too bad. Tomorrow, I'll swing you by the house to get the ring, and—"

"Wait," she says, eyes wide. "You already have it?"

"I told you, I've known for months. I've just been

waiting for you to get there with me."

Her fingers run through my hair in an affection-ate way. "I was always there with you. Still am."

"So, tomorrow it is," I tell her with a grin. "We'll have to invite my mother or I'll never hear the end of it."

"Oh no," she mutters.

"Mom likes you," I remind her. And she does. I've brought her to my parents a few times for dinner, and Mom always gives me not-so-discreet winks.

"But to spring on a courthouse wedding?"

I kiss her worried frown away and palm her still-flat stomach. "I'm giving her a daughter and a grandchild in one swoop. Mom is going to be thrilled, sweetheart."

The never-ending tension that always seems to have Jenna in its grip lessens. "This feels too good to be true."

I kiss her neck and smile against her skin. "Just let the good happen."

# eighteen

*Jenna*

"**Y**ou should see Dad's face right now," Sophia says as she enters the board-room. "All those people crammed in his office."

"All those people?" I hiss. "Like what kind of people?"

Sophia snorts. "*Your* people."

"I have people?"

Winter pushes into the room. "Man, Enzo's brother is fiiiiine."

I laugh. "Is he?" I've seen him before at Enzo's parents for dinner. He's good-looking, but Enzo is way hotter, in my opinion.

"*Your* people are pretty," Sophia agrees. "Especially that brother of his." Then she nudges me with her elbow. "But your daddy? Damn, girl."

We all giggle at that.

"Drew would be so unhappy if he heard you

gushing about my dad," I tell her with a smirk.

"The hotties from August's office are here too. Dane and Nick," Winter says, batting her lashes at me, a wicked grin on her face. "Now that's a homemade porno I wouldn't mind taking a sneak peek at."

Enzo told me they might stop by. I remember them from Christmas. Nick was the cute Santa and Dane was his handsome helper. Both are friends of Enzo's.

"The hottest people in your wedding party, though," Soph says with a pretty smile, "are us." She pulls her phone from her clutch. "Come on. Let's commemorate this moment."

The three of us squeeze together as Sophia takes a selfie. In one, we try to look our best and then the next, we make a silly face. My heart swells because it's true. I have people. It makes me ridiculously happy, too.

"How do I look?" I mutter, my nerves overtaking me.

Winter and Sophia stand side by side, spending too much time scrutinizing me. I start to feel self-conscious until they both giggle.

"Beautiful, of course," Winter says. "White's definitely your color. Take it from another ice queen. It's your color."

It's been two days since Enzo said he was going to marry me. We thought we'd show up at the courtroom the next day and get married. His mother threw a tantrum and my dad freaked about getting his mom here in time. So, we waited until my new grandma showed up and Enzo's mother took me shopping to buy a proper dress. It's simple but came from a wedding store. I even got a veil. A lot for such a simple affair. It all feels like more than I deserve.

When tears begin to swim, threatening to mess up my mascara, both of my best friends swoop in to hug me. I let them hold me and the three of us sob together. Happy tears.

"Your pregnancy emotions are contagious," Winter complains, her voice teary.

"Yeah, what the hell, J?" Sophia grumbles. "We're a bunch of crybabies now because of you."

I let out a sigh and swipe at my cheeks. "Thanks for being here."

Soph shrugs. "It beats having to be at work."

A knock at the door interrupts our giggling. Winter opens the door and my dad stands on the other side. She turns and mouths, "So hot," to me before scooting from the room. Soph smirks at me and also takes her leave. When we're alone, Dad grins at me.

"Look how beautiful you are," he praises, before pulling me in for a hug. "When I first saw you and had an inkling that you could be my daughter, I looked forward to one day walking you down the aisle. I didn't think it would ever happen, and certainly not this fast."

We both chuckle.

He pulls away to look at me. "I'm so happy we found each other."

"Me too, Dad."

"Let's do this, honey." He offers me his elbow and I take it. My heart swells. Dad is a good man. I've gotten a firsthand look at how good he is. In the way he treats me and through his actions. When I found out he was going to try and become a foster parent so he can keep Cora for me, I was more than touched. It forged an unbreakable bond between he and I. I felt that overwhelming power of a parent who'd do anything for their child—something I never thought I'd feel for myself. Even if they don't approve him or it doesn't work, the fact he tried means the world.

We walk down the hall. People who work in the courthouse buzz past us on their way to hearings or their offices, or lunch, for all I know. They whizz around, unaware that I'm about to experience the best day of my life. Dad walks me to Judge Rowe's office. The door stands open, and Sophia was right. It's crammed with *my* people. Even the ones that were Enzo's will soon be mine too.

Winter stands beside my attorney and her boyfriend, August. They are a cute couple. Beside them, Sophia and Drew are quietly arguing, both wearing wicked smiles on their faces. Enzo's mother is fussing over Enzo's tie, while his brother Eli and his father smirk nearby. Dad's mom is in a heated discussion with Judge Rowe, and every time her hand swings out as she gestures, he flinches when she nearly knocks over a picture of his family. Dane and Nick stand close, sharing knowing smiles. These people are my people.

Enzo turns and as soon as he sees me, his hazel eyes light up with love and pride. It makes me stand a little straighter. Smile a little wider. He's a wonderful man. My man. He gives me a wink and grins before mouthing, "You're beautiful."

I blush under his praise and give my dad a kiss on the cheek. "Thanks for walking me down the hallway. Way better than any church aisle."

Dad kisses my forehead. "I'd walk anywhere with you, Jenna."

He releases me and Enzo takes his place. Words are exchanged. Vows. Promises. Rings. Even a kiss. But all I see is him. All this is a show for everyone else. He's already bound to my heart. Now, it's just official.

"I love it here," I tell Enzo from my pool lounger.

"Mmmmhhmm."

I crack a smile and peek over at him. His book is

resting over his face as he steals an afternoon nap. I rake my gaze down his sculpted chest and lick my lips at seeing his dark happy trail as it dips below his waistband of his swim trunks. A happy sigh escapes me. We've been on our honeymoon to Destin, Florida for nearly a week. My dad paid for the trip as his wedding gift to us. He spared no expense either. The beachside house is the fanciest place I've ever stayed in.

My stomach grumbles and my napping husband perks up, pulling his book away to look over at me with a lifted brow. Even sleepy, he's hot. I climb out of my lounge chair and walk over to his. A smile curves his full lips up when I straddle his waist.

"You're hungry," he says, his palms settling on my hips.

"I'm always hungry," I challenge.

He smirks. "Not in the mornings. I'm not even allowed to mention breakfast."

"But it's lunchtime now. You can feed me."

His cock hardens beneath me. "I'd love to *feed* you, wife." His hazel eyes darken with lust. "After I make you some lunch."

I grind along his erection, loving the way his jaw clenches. "You could *feed* me now, husband."

He shakes his head, so I tease him. I like winning. Sitting up on my knees, I tug on one side of my bikini strap at my hip. It loosens and sags. When I do the other side, it falls into his lap. His hungry gaze slides down my stomach to my pussy. I pick up my swimsuit bottoms and toss them away.

"Jenna," he warns, his voice low and guttural. "The neighbors could see."

I untie the top of his shorts and tug them down slightly until his rock-hard cock can be pulled out the top. Our eyes are locked in a heated battle as I position myself over his tip and sink down slowly over his thick length. He lets out a hiss of pleasure, his fingers biting into my hips.

"You're a bad, bad girl."

I rock my hips. "You like it when I'm bad."

His movements are swift, and I squeal when he stands with me in his arms. He takes us inside the patio door, away from prying neighbors' eyes. We don't make it far before he pushes me up against a wall. I whimper when he nips at my throat. He rips down the cup of my swimsuit to bare my sore breast to him.

"Enzo," I cry out when he bites me again.

His hands are all over me, greedy and desperate. It makes me feel wanted and adored. I writhe at his touch. He fucks me against the wall until his breathing becomes strangled. Knowing he's close, he reaches between us and massages my clit until I'm right there with him. Together, we fall into bliss, our moans loud and unrestrained. He kisses my neck and eases me off his cock, before setting me back to my feet.

When his phone rings, he yanks up his trunks

before going to answer it, and I make my way into the bathroom. I clean up and am just coming back out when he hands me the phone.

"It's your dad," he says softly.

I frown and grab it from him. "Dad? Are you okay?"

"Hey honey," Dad replies, his voice warm and familiar and safe. This pregnancy makes me extra anxious. I find myself worrying over everyone since I found out I'm expecting. "Are you sitting down?"

The bed is nearest to me so I plop down. "I am. You're freaking me out. What's going on?"

He laughs. "Well, it looks like as soon as I take my twenty-seven-hour family resource training, I'll be ready to go."

"No," I whisper.

"Yes," he says proudly. "All the paperwork has been filed and approved. Your grandma talked to Max, and—"

"Who?"

"Judge Rowe. Anyway, she talked to him and he expedited everything. My application is approved, pending the training. But Max called to tell me I could have her by the end of the month."

I burst into tears.

Enzo sits beside me and hugs me.

"Hey," Dad says. "It's time to be happy. We're bringing her home."

I'm too overcome by emotion to say anything but, "Thank you."

"Just let the good happen, Jenna."

*Four weeks later...*

I smooth out her new quilt and then pace the floor beside Cora's bed. Enzo has gone to get her and bring her home. While he was a picture of cool, I'm a nervous wreck.

"I should be the nervous one," Dad says from her doorway. "I'm about to be a grandpa to a two-year-old."

"You're doing a great job being a dad. You've got this. But don't worry, I've got your back," I tell him with a shaky smile. I take a moment to look at him. Recently, he's been called into work a lot and I think it's taking its toll. He has dark circles under his eyes and lately, his smiles are forced. "Everything okay?"

The line between his brows deepens as he frowns. "Yeah. Just worried about one of my patients."

"Was it bad?" With him being an ER doctor, sometimes he sees some grisly patients.

"It wasn't an accident or anything. She's a recurring ER patient." He sighs and rubs at the back of his neck. "Just deteriorating is all."

I walk over to him and give him a hug. "I'm sorry."

He simply strokes my hair and rests his chin on top of my head. We stay locked in an embrace until I hear my door opening. I can hear Cora babbling to Enzo as they enter. Her sweet, adorable voice makes my heart squeeze in my chest. A few seconds later, he walks into her room with my baby on his hip.

"Mommy!" she cries out, reaching for me.

I rush over to her and pull her into my arms. Holding her tight, I press kisses all over her face, making her squeal. When I've kissed her enough and she starts squirming, I set her to her feet. She immediately makes her way over to the dollhouse Dad recently bought and starts playing. With joyful tears rolling down my cheeks, I stare happily at her as she plays.

Ever since we made the decision to stay with Dad until we can get approved to adopt Cora, we brought Halo to stay too. Halo loves the big house, and exploring. He especially likes to help Dad in the kitchen when he cooks dinner.

"Meow," Halo says blandly, peeking his head inside her room.

"Kitty!" Cora screeches, a big grin on her face. She gets to her feet and runs over to Halo. The brave cat nuzzles his head against her leg. And when she picks his heavy ass up, he just looks over at Enzo and meows as if to say, "Save me." But his tail whips back and forth contentedly, indicating he's pleased to have a playmate.

"Now that cat has someone to bug besides me," Dad says with a fake groan.

"You love my baby," Enzo says, laughing.

Dad winks at me. "Yeah, I guess I do."

"Patty said she hasn't had a nap today," Enzo whispers, when Cora starts yelling at Halo for being a bad kitty. He picks her up and she rubs at her eyes.

"I'll let you guys put her down," Dad says. "I'll be down the hall if you need me."

Once he's gone, Enzo motions to our room. Cora is already having trouble keeping her eyes open. She clings to Enzo's shirt, effectively melting my heart. We climb into our bed and put our sweet Cora in between us. She rolls toward me and twists my hair in her fingers, like old times. I smile at her and kiss her forehead. The three of us lie together quietly until her soft breathing can be heard. I yawn and drift my gaze over to Enzo. He watches me with such a loving look in his eyes.

"You're a good mom to Cora," he whispers, tucking her blonde hair behind her ear. "And you're going to be a good mom to the next one too."

I rub my slightly swollen stomach and smile. "Thanks for keeping me afloat all this time. If it weren't for you, I'd have drowned."

"Not my brave, fierce, strong wife." He leans over

Cora and kisses my lips. "You're much too tough to drown. Not to mention, you have your family and friends all around you. You're safe, Jenna. Safe and loved, and you're not going anywhere. We're not going anywhere."

I swallow down my emotions. "I don't know what to do with myself now."

His soft chuckle warms me to my soul. "Just let the good happen, sweetheart."

Closing my eyes, I let out a heavy sigh, expelling the last of my stress. I fall asleep with my baby in my belly, my Cora in my arms, and my husband in my heart.

*Just let the good happen.*

That's something I can certainly get used to.

# epilogue

*Enzo*

*One year later...*

I pat Lila's back and kiss her fuzzy brown hair. She sighs, but doesn't wake up. As I hold our baby girl, I watch Cora and Jenna from the window. These girls—each one of them—have stolen pieces of my heart. When I first met Jenna and Cora, never could I have imagined we'd end up where we are now. A family.

Cora is officially ours.

After a year of bugging the shit out of the agency, we were finally granted our most hoped-for wish. To make little Cora a Tauber. Now that she's ours, we've given Daniel his space back. He's been going through his own personal hell this past year. It'll do him some good to have us out of his hair.

I walk into Lila's nursery and lay her down. Before I leave, I stare at her for a long moment. She has my nose and eyes, but has her mother's pouty lips.

Adorable as hell and a daddy's girl. As if sharing my thoughts, she smiles in her sleep.

Slipping from her room, I make my way back into the living room. Jenna is walking in with Cora. In Cora's fist, she has a flower.

"That's a pretty flower you got there," I tell her as I kneel to inspect it.

"Flower for Daddy." She smiles at me, looking too fucking cute for words. When she'd heard Jenna refer to me as "Daddy" when talking to Lila not long after she was born, Cora decided I was her daddy then too. She doesn't really understand the whole adoption thing, but she knows her home is with Jenna and I, wherever that may be.

I kiss her forehead. "It's beautiful. Let's put it in some water."

We walk into the kitchen and I fill up a plastic cup for her. She happily stuffs the abused flower into the cup. Jenna sets to cutting up a banana, and then puts the bowl on the table for her. Cora sits in her chair, happily eating her banana.

"You okay?" I ask, pulling Jenna to me for a rare stolen quiet moment.

"Yeah, just tired. I have an exam Monday that I need to study for."

I kiss the top of her head. "Do you need to go to your dad's to study?" We may be back at my house permanently now, but I know she misses her old study.

"I might go over there for a couple of hours, if you're sure you can handle this crowd," she says, and makes a silly face at Cora.

Cora mimics her, giggles, and then shoves more banana bites into her mouth.

"If they get too out of control, I'll call Mom to come save the day," I tell her with a chuckle. My mother is a really good mother, but she's a fantastic grandma. Cora worships the ground she walks on. In the past year, when Jenna and I had to work, and Daniel would get called into the hospital, it was my mom who stepped up as babysitter for Cora. They developed a bond that's only strengthened over time.

"Your mom spoils her rotten," Jenna says, but not grumpily. She knows Cora deserves to be spoiled. The kid, like Jenna, has been through some crap. It's nice for her to get spoiled by her grandma, like every other normal kid.

Cora rubs at her face, rubbing banana all over her, and Jenna springs into action. She cleans her up and then brings her to me to let me kiss her before she lays her down for a nap. Luckily, Cora still goes down easy for her naps. A few minutes later, Jenna returns with a sly smile on her face.

"Do we have time to nap while the kids sleep?" she asks in a coy tone, before slipping from the kitchen.

I prowl after her and into our bedroom. When she peels off her shirt and shoves down her pants, my dick springs awake. Shedding my clothes along the way, I follow her into the bed. Having two little ones nearby, we've learned to be quick. I bring my wife to climax with expert speed, and then I'm reaching for a condom on the bedside table. As I put it in my teeth to tear it open, she gently takes it from me. Her green eyes blaze with love and happiness.

Arching a brow at her, I tell her with a silent expression: *We could get pregnant.*

Her smile is blindingly beautiful as she nods. *Maybe we will.*

Our mouths meet for a fervent kiss and I drive into her hard. We get lost in each other until we're both exploding with pleasure, and I fill her up with cum. The twinkle in her eyes tells me she's hoping we're successful.

"I guess we're doing this again," I murmur, before tugging her bottom lip between my teeth.

She strokes her fingers through my hair and grins. "Hopefully we'll do this again and again and again."

"Five kids?" I challenge with a chuckle.

"I want as many as you'll give me."

My cock hardens at her words, eager to fuck her at least once more today before the kids wake up. "Well then, Mrs. Tauber, we better get started." I kiss her mouth hard before pulling away to beam down at her gorgeous, happy face. "Let's make some babies, sweetheart."

**the end**

If you loved *Enzo*,
then you'll love reading Drew and Sophia's story in
*Crybaby*,
another taboo treat romance by K Webster!

# playlist

"Broken" by Lovelytheband

"Jumper" by Third Eye Blind

"Fever" by The Black Keys

"A Little Death" by The Neighbourhood

"Girls Your Age" by Transviolet

"Hatefuck" by Cruel Youth

"Walk Through the Fire" by Zayde Wolf and Ruelle

"If You Want Love" by NF

"Lie" by NF

"I Told You I Was Mean" by Ellie King

"Poison" by Meg Myers

"Middle Fingers" by Missio

"Kids Ain't All Right" by Grace Mitchell

"Carry You" by Ruelle

"Little One" by Highly Suspect

"I Don't Even Care About You" by Missio

"Heart-Shaped Box" by Dead Sara

"Numb" by Meg Myers

"Hi-Low (Hollow)" by Bishop Briggs

"The Death of Me" by Meg Myers

"Soldier" by Fleurie

"Codex" by Radiohead

"True Love Waits" by Radiohead

"High and Dry" by Radiohead

"Uninvited" by Alanis Morissette

"Him & I" by G-Eazy and Halsey

"Fade Into You" by Mazzy Star

"Animal" by Badflower

"The Sound of Silence" by Simon & Garfunkel

"Arsonist's Lullabye" by Hozier

"Work Song" by Hozier

"Hold On" by Alabama Shakes

"Hallelujah" by Jeff Buckley

"The Winding Sheet" by Mark Lanegan

"I Love You Little Girl" by Mark Lanegan

"Where Did You Sleep Last Night" by Mark Lanegan

# K Webster's taboo world

*Cast of Characters*

Brandt Smith (Rick's Best Friend)
Kelsey McMahon (Rick's Daughter)
Rick McMahon (Sheriff)
Mandy Halston (Kelsey's Best Friend)

Miles Reynolds (Drew's Best Friend)
Olivia Rowe (Max's Daughter/Sophia's Sister)

Dane Alexander (Max's Best Friend)
Nick Stratton

Judge Maximillian "Max" Rowe (Olivia and Sophia's
Father)
Dorian Dresser

Drew Hamilton (Miles's Best Friend)
Sophia Rowe (Max's Daughter/Olivia's Sister)

Easton McAvoy (Preacher)
Lacy Greenwood (Stephanie's Daughter)

Stephanie Greenwood (Lacy's Mother)
Anthony Blakely (Quinn's Son)
Aiden Blakely (Quinn's Son)

Quinn Blakely (Anthony and Aiden's Father)
Ava Prince (Lacy/Raven/Olivia's friend)

Karelma Bonilla (Mateo's Daughter)
Adam Renner (Principal)

Coach Everett Long (Adam's friend)
River Banks (Olivia's Best Friend)

Mateo Bonilla (Four Fathers Series Side Character)

Vaughn Young
Vale Young

Jenna Pruitt
Lorenzo Tauber

# K Webster's taboo world reading list

These don't necessarily have to be read in order to enjoy, but if you would like to know the order I wrote them in, it is as follows (with more being added to as I publish):

*Bad Bad Bad*
*Coach Long*
*Ex-Rated Attraction*
*Mr. Blakely*
*Malfeasance*
*Easton (Formerly known as Preach)*
*Crybaby*
*Lawn Boys*
*Renner's Rules*
*The Glue*
*Dane*
*Enzo*

# books by
# K WEBSTER

**Psychological Romance Standalones:**

*My Torin*

*Whispers and the Roars*

*Cold Cole Heart*

*Blue Hill Blood*

**Romantic Suspense Standalones:**

*Dirty Ugly Toy*

*El Malo*

*Notice*

*Sweet Jayne*

*The Road Back to Us*

*Surviving Harley*

*Love and Law*

*Moth to a Flame*

*Erased*

**Extremely Forbidden Romance Standalones:**

*The Wild*

*Hale*

**Taboo Treats:**
*Bad Bad Bad*
*Coach Long*
*Ex-Rated Attraction*
*Mr. Blakely*
*Easton*
*Crybaby*
*Lawn Boys*
*Malfeasance*
*Renner's Rules*
*The Glue*
*Dane*
*Enzo*

**Contemporary Romance Standalones:**
*The Day She Cried*
*Untimely You*
*Heath*
*Sundays are for Hangovers*
*A Merry Christmas with Judy*
*Zeke's Eden*
*Schooled by a Senior*
*Give Me Yesterday*
*Sunshine and the Stalker*
*Bidding for Keeps*
*B-Sides and Rarities*

**The V Games Series:**
*Vlad (Book 1)*
*Ven (Book 2)*
*Vas (Book 3)*

**Four Fathers Books:**
*Pearson*

**Four Sons Books:**
*Camden*

**Not Safe for Amazon Books:**
*The Wild*
*Hale*
*Bad Bad Bad*
*This is War, Baby*

**The Breaking the Rules Series:**
*Broken (Book 1)*
*Wrong (Book 2)*
*Scarred (Book 3)*
*Mistake (Book 4)*
*Crushed (Book 5—a novella)*

**The Vegas Aces Series:**
*Rock Country (Book 1)*
*Rock Heart (Book 2)*
*Rock Bottom (Book 3)*

**The Becoming Her Series:**
*Becoming Lady Thomas (Book 1)*
*Becoming Countess Dumont (Book 2)*
*Becoming Mrs. Benedict (Book 3)*

**Alpha & Omega Duet:**
*Alpha & Omega (Book 1)*
*Omega & Love (Book 2)*

# acknowledgements

Thank you to my husband. You're my hero! I love you for all that you do and all that you are!

A huge thank you to my Krazy for K Webster's Books reader group. You all are insanely supportive and I can't thank you enough.

A gigantic thank you to those who always help me out. Elizabeth Clinton, Ella Stewart, Misty Walker, Holly Sparks, Jillian Ruize, Gina Behrends, Jessica Hollyfield, Ker Dukey, and Nikki Ash—you ladies are my rock!

Thank you so much to Misty Walker for keeping me grounded when I float too high and for lifting me up when I get too low. I love you like a sister!

Thank you Teresa Nicholson for lending your eagle eyes to me in a pinch!

A big thank you to my author friends who have given me your friendship and your support. You have no idea how much that means to me.

A huge thank you to my "angels"! (Although y'all

would like to argue you're not so sweet ha!) Thank you for taking a chance on something new with me and reading/reviewing the book early! You are all heaven sent!

Thank you to all of my blogger friends both big and small that go above and beyond to always share my stuff. You all rock! #AllBlogsMatter

Thanks Jenn from All About the Edits for editing my story!

Thank you Stacey Blake for being amazing as always when formatting my books and in general. I love you! I love you! I love you!

A big thanks to my PR gal, Nicole Blanchard. You are fabulous at what you do and keep me on track!

Lastly but certainly not least of all, thank you to all of the wonderful readers out there who are willing to hear my story and enjoy my characters like I do. It means the world to me!

# about the author

K Webster is the *USA Today* bestselling author of over seventy romance books in many different genres including contemporary romance, historical romance, paranormal romance, dark romance, romantic suspense, taboo romance, and erotic romance. When not spending time with her hilarious and handsome husband and two adorable children, she's active on social media connecting with her readers.

Her other passions besides writing include reading and graphic design. K can always be found in front of her computer chasing her next idea and taking action. She looks forward to the day when she will see one of her titles on the big screen.

Join K Webster's newsletter to receive a couple of updates a month on new releases and exclusive content. To join, all you need to do is go here (www. authorkwebster.com).

Facebook:
www.facebook.com/authorkwebster

Blog:
authorkwebster.wordpress.com

Twitter:
twitter.com/KristiWebster

Email:
kristi@authorkwebster.com

Goodreads:
www.goodreads.com/user/show/10439773-k-webster

Instagram:
instagram.com/kristiwebster

# K WEBSTER'S
*Taboo World*

two interconnected stories

BAD
BAD
BAD

two taboo treats

k webster

# *Bad Bad Bad*

Two interconnected stories. Two taboo treats.

Brandt's Cherry Girl

He's old enough to be her father.
She's his best friend's daughter.
Their connection is off the charts.
And so very, very wrong.
This can't happen.
Oh, but it already is…

Sheriff's Bad Girl

He's the law and follows the rules.
She's wild and out of control.
His daughter's best friend is trouble.
And he wants to punish her…
With his teeth.

USA TODAY BESTSELLING AUTHOR
K WEBSTER
She's a hurdle in his way...
and he wants to jump her.
a taboo treat
COACH
LONG

# *Coach Long*

Coach Everett Long has a chip on his shoulder.
Working every day with the man who stole his
fiancée leaves him pissed and on edge.
His temper is volatile and his attitude sucks.

River Banks is a funky-styled runner
with a bizarre past.
Starting over at a new school was supposed to
be easy…but she should have known better.
She likes to antagonize and tends to go after
what she's not supposed to have.

When the arrogant bully meets the strong-willed
brat, it sparks an illicit attraction.
Together, they heat up the track with
longing and desire.
Everything about their chemistry is wrong.
So why does it feel so right?

She's a hurdle in his way and, dear God does
he want to jump her.
Will she be worth the risk or
will he fall flat on his face?

# *Ex-Rated Attraction*

I liked Caleb.

I like his dad more.

Miles Reynolds sent shocks through me the very first time I met him. With his full beard and sculpted ass, he's every inch a heroic, powerful Greek god.

He saved me from a bad situation and now he's all I can think of. Every minute of every hour of every day, I want that man.

He's warned me away, says I can't handle what he has to give.

But I know better.

Miles is exactly what I need—now, then and forever.

## *Mr. Blakely*

It started as a job.

It turned into so much more.

Mr. Blakely is strict with his sons, but he's soft and gentle with me.

The powerful businessman is something else entirely when we're together.

Boss, teacher, lover…husband.

My hopes and dreams for the future have changed. I want—no, I need—him by my side.

*a taboo treat*

# malfeasance

Judge Rowe
never had
a problem with
morality...
*until her.*

USA TODAY BESTSELLING AUTHOR

# K WEBSTER

# *Malfeasance*

Max Rowe always follows the rules.
A successful judge.
A single father.
A leader in the community.
Doing the right thing means everything.

But when he finds himself rescuing an incredibly
young woman,
everything he's worked hard for is quickly forgotten.
The only thing that matters is keeping her safe.
She's gorgeous, intelligent, and the ultimate
temptation.
Doing the wrong thing suddenly feels right.

Their chemistry is intense.
It's a romance no one will approve of, yet one they
can't ignore.
Hot, fast, and explosive.
Someone is going to get burned.

He'll give up everything for her...
because without her, he is nothing.

# EASTON

## K WEBSTER

# *Easton*

A man who made countless mistakes.
A woman with a messy past.

He's tasked with helping her find her way.
She's lost in grief and self-doubt.

Together they begin something innocent…
Until it's not.

His freedom is at risk.
Her heart won't survive another break.

All rational thinking says they
should stay away from each other.
But neither are very good
at following the rules.

A deep, dark craving.
An overwhelming need.
A burn much hotter than any hell
they could ever be condemned to.

He'll give up everything for her...
because without her, he is nothing.

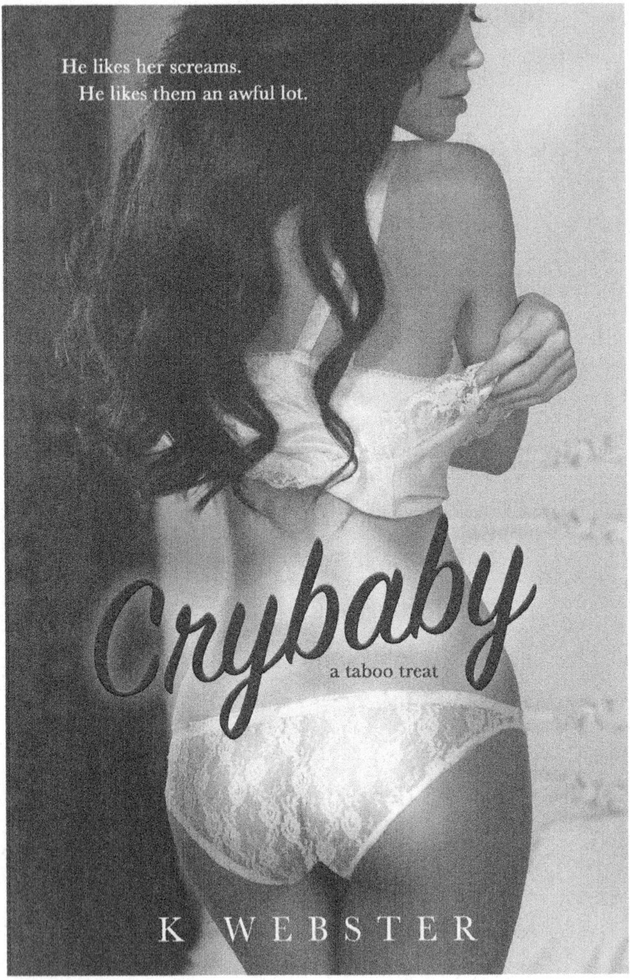
He likes her screams.
He likes them an awful lot.
Crybaby
a taboo treat
K WEBSTER

# *Crybaby*

Stubborn.
Mouthy.
Brazen.
Two people with vicious tongues.
A desperate temptation neither can ignore.

An injury has changed her entire life.
She's crippled, hopeless, and angry.
And the only one who can lessen her pain is him.

Being the boss is sometimes a pain in the ass.
He's irritated, impatient, and doesn't play games.
Yet he's the only one willing to fight her…for her.

Daring.
Forbidden.
Out of control.
Someone is going to get hurt.
And, oh, how painfully sweet that will be.

The grass is greener where
he points his hose...

# lawn
# BOYS

*a taboo treat*

USA TODAY BESTSELLING AUTHOR
# K WEBSTER

# *Lawn Boys*

She's lived her life and it has been a good one.
Marriage. College. A family.
Slowly, though, life moved forward and left her at a
standstill.

Until the lawn boy barges into her world.
Bossy. Big. Sexy as hell.
A virile young male to remind her she's all woman.

Too bad she's twice his age.
Too bad he doesn't care.

She's older and wiser and more mature.
Which means absolutely nothing when he's invading
her space.

USA TODAY BESTSELLING AUTHOR

K WEBSTER

Principal Renner,
I've been *bad*.
Again.

*a taboo treat*

# RENNER'S
*Rules*

# Renner's Rules

I'm a bad girl.
I was sent away.
New house. New rules. New school.
Change was supposed to be…good.

Until I met him.

No one warned me Principal Renner would be so
hot.
I'd expected some old, graying man in a brown suit.
Not this.
Not well over six feet of lean muscle and piercing
green eyes.
Not a rugged-faced, ax-wielding lumberjack of a
man.

He's grouchy and rude and likes to boss me around.
I find myself getting in trouble just so he'll punish
me.
Especially with his favorite metal ruler.

Being bad never felt so good

USA TODAY BESTSELLING AUTHOR
K WEBSTER
Two people.
Their unraveling
marriage.
And they want
me to be...
the
GLUE
a taboo treat

## *The Glue*

I'm a fixer. A lover. Always searching for the right fit.
And I come up empty every time.
My desires are unusual.
I don't feel whole until I'm in the middle, holding it
all together.
Which makes having a romantic relationship really
difficult.

Until them.
Two people. An unraveling marriage. Love on the
rocks.
And they want me.
To put them back together again.

Problem is, once they're fixed, where does that leave
me?
I sure as hell hope I stick like glue.

USA TODAY BESTSELLING AUTHOR

# K WEBSTER

He was the boss in
the bedroom.
I was the boss outside of it.
Two alphas.
One hot agenda.

# DANE

*a taboo treat*

I'm used to being in charge.
In the courtroom. In life. In the bedroom.
But then I met him.

He brings me *literally* to my knees.

Handsome. Charismatic. Sexy as hell.
He's everything I desperately crave to possess.

I'm burning to get him beneath me just to have a
taste.
Turns out, though, one taste isn't enough.
And he's starved for me too.

Two alphas fighting for dominance.
He thrives on control and I can't give it up.

A battle of wills.
The bedroom is the battlefield and our hearts are on
the line.

USA TODAY BESTSELLING AUTHOR

# K WEBSTER

SHE DOESN'T NEED
A HERO.
SHE JUST NEEDS
HIM.

# en
# zo

A TABOO TREAT

Jenna's grown up in the system.
Forced to be tough, wary, and hard.

She's only been able to count on herself.
Until Enzo.
He's much older and responsible for looking after her.
What should be a job to him, evolves into much
more.

Late night phone calls.
Lingering touches.
A forbidden fire that burns brighter each day.

Everything about him exudes strength.
His will to protect her is more than she could ever
ask for.
Sadly, though, even heroes have their limitations.

But she doesn't need a hero.
She just needs him.

Made in the USA
Monee, IL
06 August 2021